Ebenezer Ward

The South-Eastern Disctrict of South Australia

SALZWASSER
VERLAG

Ebenezer Ward

The South-Eastern Disctrict of South Australia

1st Edition | ISBN: 978-3-75250-412-5

Place of Publication: Frankfurt am Main, Germany

Year of Publication: 2020

Salzwasser Verlag GmbH, Germany.

Reprint of the original, first published in 1869.

THE

SOUTH-EASTERN DISTRICT

OF

South Australia.

ITS

RESOURCES AND REQUIREMETS.

BY

EBENEZER WARD,

AUTHOR OF "THE VINEYARDS AND ORCHARDS OF SOUTH AUSTRALIA," &c., &c.

REPRINTED WITH EMENDATIONS AND ADDITIONS FROM LETTERS WRITTEN EXPRESSLY FOR

"The South Australian Advertiser" and "Weekly Chronicle and Mail" Newspapers.

ADELAIDE :

PUBLISHED BY THE AUTHOR AT THE OFFICES OF *The South Australian,* NEWSPAPER,

107, KING WILLIAM STREET, (OPPOSITE THE TOWN HALL.)

MOUNT GAMBIER—LAURIE, WATSON, & LAURIE, Commercial-Road, East.
PENOLA—MR. S. MACKENZIE.   NARRACOORTE—MR. H. T. JONES.
MELBOURNE—GEO. ROBERTSON.   LONDON ... S. W. SILVER & CO.

1869.

DEDICATED,

BY PERMISSION,

TO

GEORGE WOODROFFE GOYDER, ESQUIRE,

Surveyor-General of the Province of South Australia,

AS AN ACKNOWLEDGMENT OF HIS

INTEREST IN THE

WELFARE OF THE SOUTH-EASTERN DISTRICT GENERALLY,

AND OF HIS PROMOTION OF WORKS CALCULATED

TO RECLAIM A LARGE AREA OF

UNPRODUCTIVE LAND,

THEREBY FACILITATING THE OCCUPATION OF THE COUNTRY

AND HASTENING THE DEVELOPMENT

OF ITS RESOURCES.

PREFACE.

———◇◇◇———

I wish some one would burst the fetters imposed by the fashion of prefaces. What ought there to be said in a preface? Surely without one a book should be complete in itself. At all events, I may be reticent here respecting the present volume, for its contents have already been introduced to the public in another form. It will, I hope, be of some value in disseminating information about an interesting and important district of South Australia, now too little known to the public generally. With this one aspiration, I leave it to its fate.

I gladly avail myself, also, of this opportunity to acknowledge the unvarying courtesy and kindness extended to me by the settlers in the South-East, with whom I was brought into contact during my wanderings in connection with this work.

EBENEZER WARD.

WHITMORE TERRACE, NORTH ADELAIDE,
JUNE 1ST, 1869.

INDEX.

CHAPTER IX.

CHAPTER X.

CHAPTER XI.

CHAPTER XII.

INTRODUCTORY.

It is a maxim that the more people learn the more they become impressed with a sense of their own comparative ignorance. Ideas based only upon supposition are too often found wofully wanting when weighed in the balances of reality and fact, and most of our structures of the imagination are shattered by their first contact with the materialism of things as they are. In my present position I am fully able to supply another illustration of these truths. When I undertook to visit and report upon the South-Eastern District in the capacity of a "special correspondent" my notions of the task before me fell a long way short of the conception of it which a month's observation has forced me to entertain. I have found from day to day good reason to enlarge the basis upon which I originally designed to put together a series of descriptive notes, and now, on the threshold of the narration of what I have seen and learned, I am far more doubtful of being able to do justice to the subject than I was when I knew nothing, practically, about it. I shall endeavor, however, as fully and clearly as I can to describe the district as I have found it, and to indicate not merely what in my own opinion is necessary to promote its development and prosperity, but the various views on that point which are entertained by different sections of its population. These of course may be divided and subdivided, not alone by the diverging channels in which human thought will run, but by the various interests which are established, and the separate points of their location. Unanimity of sentiment is certainly not yet characteristic of the South-Eastern people; but it is, perhaps, not too much to hope that by the future legislative treatment of this rich and interesting portion of the colony, we may succeed, in a greater degree than we have done in the past, in fusing together and consolidating the interests which its resources are calculated to support; and then, at all events, we may anticipate more harmony of purpose and opinion than prevails at present. As it is, it would be folly to expect that whatever arguments I may deduce from what I have seen, or even the conclusions I may venture to draw of the future advancement of the district, will harmonise with all the shades of party and local feeling which exist. But—"give me leave to speak my mind."

It is necessary in these introductory remarks to indicate the plan upon which I purpose dealing with my subject. I have acquired chiefly from personal observation, but partly from information and statistical research, a great array of facts, illustrative of the natural resources of the district, and the present progress of their development. I have also endeavored to make myself acquainted with its wants, by which I mean its just claims upon the fostering care of Government. I intend, first of all, to divide my articles, as it were, by the natural boundaries of the localities to which they will specially refer, and to deal separately with the distinct although kindred subjects of capabilities and requirements. I shall therefore reserve what I may have to urge respecting the measures necessary to ensure the full development of the district as a whole, and its actual as well as nominal attachment to South Australia, until I have completed all I have to write about it in a merely descriptive sense.

One other prefatory remark and I will go straight to the work before me. It is this. Residents in the South-Eastern District, who will no doubt look with some little interest for these papers, or even frequent visitors there to whom its resources and its vast wealth of natural phenomena are already familiar, must not suppose that I set out with any idea of writing anything descriptively that will be new to them. It very often happens that people who live among the scenes a writer attempts to describe estimate his success rather by the fecundity of his imagination than by his exactness of relation. Many a painstaking and conscientious effort of the kind has been dismissed with the inconsiderate criticism of "Oh, we knew all that before." My stay in the district has been limited to six weeks, and as many of its inhabitants have resided there more than three times as many years, they must not complain if of all I write "what is true isn't new;" and for my part, I hope I shall avoid justifying the application of the reverse of the phrase. The South-Eastern District is, however, absolutely and entirely unknown, except by report, to nine-tenths of the population of the colony of which it forms a part, and that fact alone would justify the publication of the present series of articles in a newspaper devoted to the interests of the province as a whole, and I hope their reproduction in this form. But I trust, too, that the wider dissemination of a knowledge of the district, and especially of the opportunities it offers for the prosperous settlement of a far larger population than it sustains at present, will, to some extent, have the beneficial effect of promoting and stimulating more comprehensive efforts than have hitherto been made by the Legislature to realise its full value to South Australia.

CHAPTER I.

SOME GENERAL OBSERVATIONS.—THE ROUTE TO THE SOUTH-EAST.

IT is a significant but unfortunate fact that we no sooner set foot in what is known as the South-Eastern District than we encounter an absurd and mischievous anomaly in legislation. Its present boundaries, for Parliamentary representation and all public purposes, extend from the River Murray on the west and north to the mouth of the Glenelg on the south, from which point an arbitrary line running due north to the Murray separates not only the district, but South Australia, from the colony of Victoria. These are, in fact, the boundary lines of our electoral district of Victoria, and on two sides out of four they are about as ill-adapted for the purpose as any that could be designed. If all the country comprised within those limits were good and habitable, its very extent would compel a subdivision for all purposes of local self-government and representation. But as it is it is simply impossible either to govern equitably or to represent adequately such a district by any local agency. The great desert, which extends almost from Wellington to the Reedy Creek Swamps, is an unconquerable natural barrier to all community of purpose and identity of interest between the

north-western and south-eastern extremities of the district. In fact, the connection of Wellington, the Lake Albert peninsula, and all the country northward to the Murray, with the South-East, is merely nominal and political. It is true that but for the Wellington votes at the last general election the district would have been deprived of the services of the best member it has ever had, but that was the direct consequence of the accidental circumstance of the two principal grounds of political contest in the district being identical with those which divided the public action of the whole colony at the time, and certainly not because of the existence of any purely local sympathy between Wellington and Penola. Let me give one practical instance of the absurdity of the boundaries. There is a local auxiliary branch of the Destitute Board for the South-Eastern District, which very properly sits at Mount Gambier as the present centre of population. A pauper at Wellington requiring State relief must apply to the Mount Gambier Board for the Government ration ! Again, a Hospital for the South-Eastern District is being built at Mount Gambier, and to it cases arising on the eastern side of the Murray will have to be sent. I might multiply instances of the kind, but it is scarcely necessary to do so. Still, as I can only regard Wellington as nominally attached to the South-East, and I shall scarcely have occasion to refer to it again, it is as well to have explained at once the incongruity and practical inconvenience of the present boundaries. It may be as well too, before entering the region of local detail, to give a few general statistical proofs of the progress of the whole district, as foreshadowing the present importance of the interests I shall have to deal with. In 1861 the population of the entire district was 5,466, and in 1866 it had risen to 9,300. In 1861 the land alienated from the Crown was 184,587 acres, and in 1866, 397,087. There were 7,560 acres under cultivation in 1861, and 23,123 in 1866. Of these 4,463 were under wheat in 1861, and 13,623 in 1866. The produce therefrom (in grain alone) was 117,153 bushels in 1861, and 246,127 in 1866. There were 6,987 horses in the district in 1861, and 12,247 in 1866, and although the cattle depastured there had decreased from 57,007 in 1861 to 34,551 in 1866, the sheep had increased in the same period from 819,104 to 1,300,786, and the wool exported from Guichen Bay and Port MacDonnell, exclusive of shipments coastwise to Port Adelaide, had risen from 2,067,240 lbs. in 1861 to 2,537,250 lbs. in 1866. These figures indicate a power of expansion which would be respectable if even it were approaching its limit, but as it is now manifestly only in the infancy of its development I know of no better claim I can adduce to the attention and interest of the public generally for the tale I am going to unfold.

And now for the road ! The means of communication between two points 300 miles apart, but having in any respect a common interest, is necessarily a question of importance. There are two established lines between which travellers to the South-East may choose ; one by overland mail three times a week ; the other by the Penola steamer to Guichen Bay and Port MacDonnell once a fortnight. The latter requires no comment, for coasting voyages in steamers are fully understood ; and if even they were not, I should be loth to suggest unpalatable ideas to such of my readers as may have tender stomachs. But about the overland line a few words are necessary to the completeness of these papers. It is certainly creditable to both Government and the mail contractors that a journey which little more than six months ago occupied nearly five days, is now performed efficiently in two, but I do not despair of the distance being eventually accomplished in eight or ten hours less. I left Adelaide for my trip on Saturday, the 18th of May. The mail is advertised to leave the General Post-Office at 10.30 p.m., and at 15 minutes past the hour precisely I was there duly equipped and eager for a start. But mail drivers are sometimes curiously independent of all will but their own. They are capital fellows in their way, but generally they display quite a sufficient sense of the essential character of their services. While I was in the booking-office, securing, as I fondly thought, a " seat," the maildriver having obtained the bags from the Post-Office, gallopped off just 10 minutes before his time, to the bewilderment of the Booking Clerk, and the dismay of one or two other people interested in the proceeding. For my own part, I felt very much like being left behind, and so I should have been, but that " a friend in need is a friend indeed." I had been driven to the Post-Office by a gentleman whose general philanthropy is only equalled by the versatility of his talent and the fastness and energy of his action; and if to this I add that he is one of the members for Onkaparinga, I shall sufficiently indicate him. "In chase of the mail" was a chance not to be foregone. While the worthy proprietor of the coach that had gone was still scratching his head in perplexity, my honorable friend had gathered up his ribbons, and we were both settled for the race. An admonitory word or two to the sleek black mare and we were "off." How we swung round certain corners, and didn't knock down unwary pedestrians as we tore through the labyrinth of narrow streets which are supposed to afford a near cut to the Glen Osmond road, I never knew. Once on a clear course, my friend's ecstacy was perfect, and we rattled along merrily at a pace that must have astonished the stately municipal trees which line the road, if it wouldn't even have beaten Cowra for the Cup. I could almost fancy as those graceful gums flitted past us in the bright moonlight that they bowed their high tops to the spirit of ex-Mayoralty that was careering through them. Now a dark form looms ahead, and by the lights it bears we know it is the mail. A minute more and we are past it; but there is no such thing as pulling up on the post. Blood is up, and a merry gallop for another mile was the least that would satisfy my friend and his mare. I have recorded the incident for the double purpose of acknowledging my indebtedness to the "honorable member," and as a hint to South-Eastern travellers who may not have so good a friend at hand when mail drivers are more than punctual. About the ride from Adelaide to Milang little need be said, except that the distance is about 50 miles, and that the ground is got over in five hours and a

half. Formerly the route was by Wellington, and through the "Fourteen-mile Desert;" but now a welcome change has been effected for the smooth waters and cheerful aspect of Lakes Alexandrina and Albert. You leave the coach upon the shore of Lake Alexandrina, and to the traveller who for a whole night has been vainly endeavoring to sleep in spite of fate—as represented by the perpetual jolting incidental to any conveyances as yet extant, and the corkscrew position in which the pressure of mail-bags, and other "unavoidable circumstances," necessitate the adjustment of one's limbs—the opportunity to stretch himself out and yawn without restriction becomes a very luxury of life. You may do this to your heart's content while the mails are being made up at the Milang Post-Office; and then you must tramp along the narrow jetty, where you will find the L.A.S.N.Co.'s steamer Telegraph with steam up ready to receive you, and an attentive steward overrunning with very welcome suggestions about hot coffee and grilled kidneys. I pity the man who cannot appreciate even the remembrance of such things at such a time. Indeed, this Lake trip is one of the greatest improvements of all that have been introduced in the overland mail service. Of course mails must be considered first, but in this case there is some gain of time in the transmission of Her Majesty's letter-bags, and an unspeakable degree of comfort ensured to passengers as compared with the dreary and unbroken ride through the desert that is now escaped. The run across to Meningie occupies about five hours, and during this time passengers may enjoy a comfortable sleep, a good breakfast, and a most refreshing wash, besides gladdening all their sense of beauty and veneration with the sight of a sunrise on the lakes. The business of disembarking mails and passengers at Meningie is accomplished—in the absence of a jetty—in a somewhat primitive fashion, and a story, which is likely to grow into a legend, is current here about the appearance presented recently by a late "Hon. Chief Secretary" as he was borne by a diminutive but sturdy A.B. (seaman) "pig-a-back" from the steamer to the shore.

CHAPTER II.

Although Meningie is still only in the first year of its existence as a "township," it affords already significant evidences of its future importance. Two "houses of accommodation".—I can scarcely say hotels—are established there, and, as settlement progresses in the neighborhood, there will be quite sufficient enterprise to supply other legitimate requirements. With the usual fatality of official action, a bungle seems to have been made in fixing the site of the town, and the settlers there, or some of them, complain very bitterly of the error. Where the town has been placed the water is shallow at the landing-place, but at some little distance away much deeper water can be obtained close to the shore, and here it is supposed the jetty will have to be erected. There would thus be a gap between the landing-place and the town, which ought even now to be avoided, if that be possible. There is some very fair land on the flats bordering the lake

about Meningie, but directly you leave the township on the Coorong side a dreary belt of mallee scrub commences. This is, indeed, the western extremity of the Desert. It has one peculiarity in the retentive character of its soil in large patches of it. On the rises sand prevails, but on all the hollows or flats there is a kind of white pipeclay, and this is frequently quite destitute of even scrub vegetation. A more cheerless expanse can scarcely be conceived, and when you emerge from it upon the open flats of the Coorong, and trace the rippling waters of the stream winding their way in a broad open channel parallel with the track you are following, it is impossible to avoid condemning the obstinacy which has so long prevented that fine sheet of water being utilised for the purposes of navigation. It has been shown over and over again by practical men who have a personal knowledge of the stream, and all its impediments, that the expenditure of a very few thousand pounds would render it permanently navigable to Salt Creek for such a steamer as that which now works so efficiently and usefully on the Lakes. It is by the present land route nearly 40 miles from Meningie to Salt Creek, and the whole of this distance may just as well be done by the steamer as the run across the Lakes, when the few obstructions which exist have been removed. What the gain in comfort and rest would be to mail passengers may be fairly estimated from the experiences of the present shorter smoothwater steaming to Meningie, and besides this the value of all the country on the Coorong would be largely increased by affording the settlers there the cheapest of all roads for their goods traffic. At present the cargo boats are uncertain in their passages and sometimes have to be discarded altogether, but a mail steamer running as I suggest could easily tow goods barges even when " on service." I am glad to know that the project will be fairly tested soon, and its success, about which I have no doubts at all, will be one more link in the chain which is destined I hope to unite inseparably the interests of Adelaide and the South-East.

Very little requires to be said about the country from the Coorong to near Lacepede Bay. Of the stream itself I need only add to what I have written that its depth of water is chiefly affected by the winds, and that when it rises to its greatest height it spreads over a much wider surface than its channel proper occupies. But in that channel there is always water enough for the purposes I have indicated, except at two or three places where "bars" will have to be cut through. On the seaward side of the stream there is a narrow strip of country, chiefly sandhills, and on the inland side a still narrower strip of open flats and dry

sheaoak ridges alternately, beyond which lies the fatal scrub. This last-named strip, which runs all the way parallel with the Coorong and the coast-line, and rarely exceeds half a mile in width, is very properly reserved for travelling stock. There are public-houses at Magrath's Flat, Wood's Wells (where the grave of Malachi Martin's victim is still pointed out to travellers), Chinaman's Wells, and Salt Creek. Along most of this distance, when the Coorong is at its lowest, and the outer edges of its bed are dry, you have a splendid road upon its hard pipeclay bottom, and passengers are then often warmed out of their resignation to " mail miseries," by the excitement of a slashing gallop over the too tempting course. When the stream is higher this luxury is impracticable, and you must, instead, plod drearily along the sandy track on the ridges, and the slushy surface of the flats. At Salt Creek the Coorong loses itself in a wide extent of swamp, which penetrates the scrub almost uninterruptedly to the Reedy Creek waters eastward of Lacepede Bay. It will be important to remember this fact in connection with Mr. Goyder's scheme for the drainage of the South-East, to which I shall have presently to refer. Coolatoo is the first stage after leaving Salt Creek, and at the changing place beyond it, some cultivation for horse-feed has been carried on successfully. The road beyond that lies for the most part along a dry ridge of light soil, sparsely timbered, and at about eight miles north of Lacepede Bay, the traveller once more finds himself amongst cultivated paddocks and farm homesteads. The settlements, although neither numerous nor extensive, are sufficient to prove the suitability of the soil for agricultural settlement, and to illustrate the injustice of the prejudice which somehow or another has become the fashion against the capabilities of the land about Lacepede Bay. I am not going to overrate those capabilities; but, notwithstanding the contrary opinion which has been gradually nursed into conviction, and is now, I know, widely entertained, I shall state plainly the truth as I found it.

This ridge on which cultivation is now progressing runs parallel with the coast line, due north and south, from about 15 miles north of Lacepede Bay to the foot of the Mount Benson range, some 15 miles to the southward of the township. It is bounded on the west by the sandhills of the coast, except that in places the ridge itself dips almost to the beach. Its width varies from seven or eight miles near Mount Benson, to about a mile, or even less at places, being skirted on the eastward for its entire length, firstly, by the swamps running into the Coorong at Salt Creek; then by the Maria Creek Swamp at Lacepede Bay; and, finally, by the Biscuit Flat at the Mount Benson end. Now I am far from classing all this soil as of first-class quality, and no doubt by comparison with the strong clays of Penola, the fine black loams of Kalangadoo, and the exceptionally rich volcanic soil of Mount Gambier, it sinks to inferiority. But, on the other hand, compared with the bulk of the lands farmed in less-favored parts of the colony, it is of quite an average quality, and may be pronounced for the most part fair arable land, not very expensive to clear, easily worked, and with a far better climate for the growth of root crops and cereals than the more northern districts of the colony possess. The soil is a light warm sandy loam, resting on a limestone formation. It is undulating, well grassed, and lightly timbered with sheaoak and honeysuckle; but on the southern end of the ridge, at the spur of the Mount Benson Range, trending to the sea, the soil has more consistency and tenacity, and is altogether stronger land, more expensive to work, and probably more productive. The swamps on the eastward of the northern or Adelaide end of this ridge are scarcely likely to be reclaimed, even by the drainage, beyond being rendered available to some extent for grazing purposes; but the Maria Creek Swamp offers a fine field for enterprise and industry. I have no doubt this opinion will be demurred to by very many whose prejudices or want of personal knowledge on the subject may impair their judgment; but let the facts speak for themselves. The surface soil upon this swamp, which varies in depth from six inches to three and four feet, is a black vegetable mould, resulting from the continual decomposition of the super-abundant vegetation it produces. On some slight rises which occur, where there has been less water and finer grasses, decomposition is more advanced on and near the surface than it is in the hollows where the water has stood longer, and there has been ranker and coarser vegetation left to decay, almost untouched by the cattle that have grazed down the grasses on the drier spots. Here too, as a natural consequence, the soil is less consolidated, and as you walk upon it, you sink ankle deep into the spongy mass. Below this vegetable mould, there is a considerable depth of a white calcareous clay, plentifully studded, as is also the surface mould, with minute shells. Until now, this swamp, which extends in a southerly direction until it merges into the Biscuit Flat, has been covered with water in every wet season. A cutting was made about a year ago, running across the swamp in a due east and west line. The stuff taken out of it was used for forming the embankment of a road which is in fact the main line to Narracoorte, and has only just now been completed. Less regard appears to have been had to the completeness of the cutting than to the requirements of the embankment, and the channel is in a quite unfinished state, and at some places is little more than a very irregular series of holes. Still, incomplete as it is, it has been of considerable service in materially reducing the waters on the swamp, and giving them an outlet into the creek, instead of their being dammed back on the eastward, and confined as formerly to a tedious escape by their natural fall to the north-west. This is all that has been done up to the present time for the drainage of the northern end of the district, but it is of signal value in indicating the grand results which remain to be accomplished. I take it to be an established fact that the drainage system, which has been ably designed and is now being most energetically carried out by Mr. Goyder,* is capable of a thoroughly successful application to all parts of the district, and that by a judicious and reasonable expenditure it may be made the means of reclaiming a vast extent of remarkably rich soil, and of converting a dreary waste of water into a very paradise of profitable settlement and national prosperity. It would be departing from the system I have laid down for the compilation of these articles to go fully into the details of the drainage scheme at this point, which in the present stage of its development affects almost exclusively the Penola, German Flat, and Mount Muirhead Districts. But, inasmuch as Mr. Goyder intends to deal quite separately with the drainage of this northern end, and will actually commence the work as soon as all the necessary levels can be

taken, it will be as well to explain now what it is intended to do there. So far as present observations have gone it is proposed to make two outlets at the northern end of the district, one at Lacepede Bay into Maria Creek, which will drain the Maria Creek Swamp, and all the Biscuit Flat north of the Mount Benson range; and another into the Coorong at Salt Creek, which will drain the whole extent of the Avenue Flats lying to the eastward of the Maria Creek Swamp, and uniting with several other flats at Reedy Creek, and falling thence to Salt Creek, as others do from Blackford to Maria Creek. Thus these two points—the Salt Creek having an outlet into the Coorong, and Maria Creek having an outlet 50 miles further south to Lacepede Bay—will, in fact, tap the whole waters of the northern end of the district. The levels which have been already taken establish the efficiency of this scheme; and all the borings that have been made show that the levels of the bottoms of the proposed cuttings either reach or are below the ordinary water level. The area of the drains will depend upon the maximum rainfall calculated to occur during any 24 hours, but it is already ascertained that they will in any case be of sufficient capacity to be available for navigation. Now, then, I can bring these conditions of the scheme to a focus in so far as they affect the Maria Creek Swamp, with the capabilities of which, as they will be developed by drainage, I am especially dealing. First of all, the drains will relieve the land, not only of the waters which now flow over it from the higher levels to the southward, but also of its own superabundant rainfall which the soil will not absorb. Secondly, the drain which will be cut parallel with the course of the swamp from south to north, to tap the

* The Surveyor-General of South Australia.

present east and west cutting into the creek, will be capable of serving either of the two useful purposes of navigation, or irrigation, if necessary. It will be as easy to conserve, and utilise these waters by allowing them to overflow the adjacent lands periodically, as it is to " warp," as it is called, the potato lands on the banks of rivers in Oxfordshire and Yorkshire. And when this is done what is there to prevent what is now the waste of the Maria Creek Swamp becoming the Warrnambool of South Australia? I am sure no better land can be found for the cultivation of the potato than the rich vegetable mould and clay subsoil of this swamp, when it is drained, especially if the means of copious irrigation at will are retained. Add to this that the climate is eminently suitable, and that there is perfect immunity from the frosts which render the cultivation of this valuable crop too hazardous to be profitable at Mount Gambier, and the most sceptical should be satisfied. Already one resident at Kingston, Mr. J. Bartleet, has raised a splendid sample of potatoes upon this very soil, and as they were actually dug when I was at the Bay, and are of the finest quality and size, the possibility of developing a vast resource of wealth in this direction alone can scarcely be disputed. And another thing to be remembered is that this rich potato-ground of the future is immediately adjacent to what is admitted on all hands to be a first-class natural harbor.

There is something more to be said about the "available" country in the immediate vicinity of Lacepede Bay. I have already described the coast ridge, and the swamps running parallel with it on its inland side. Now I must ask my readers to follow me in a due easterly line towards the Reedy Creek.

Beyond the Maria Creek Swamp, on the eastward, there is a wide expanse of country, varying with extreme regularity from wet flats and teatree swamps to scrubby rises and occasional banks of dry, light soil, well grassed and thinly timbered. The rises increase in altitude as you go eastward, and are sandy on most of the highest points, until the ridge from which you descend to the Reedy Creek acquires almost the importance of a range. [I shall describe the country further eastward than this when I come to my Narracoorte Chapters.] Now of all this land lying between the Reedy Creek and the Maria Creek Swamp, and extending almost as far south as the Mount Benson Range, only a comparatively small portion is fit for immediate agricultural settlement. A good section, or even a series of sections, could be selected here and there, but an arable "district" sufficiently extensive to command all the advantages of settlement and means of communication and traffic could hardly be found under existing conditions. The flats, especially on the Murrabinna country, are well adapted for cattle, now when the waters are down, but they will be of no greater value until drained. Then the whole extent of them will be converted into valuable pastoral or agricultural country. There is not on all parts of these flats the same depth of black mould as on the Maria Creek Swamp, and what soil there is is not so rich in decaying vegetable substances. In some places, too, limestone crops out on the surface, and at others the ground is strongly impregnated with salt. The latter instances are, however, exceptional, and the greater portion of all these flats is fairly reclaimable for agricultural purposes, and what is not will be vastly improved as pasture land by the works that are proposed. The surface soil of the timbered ridges varies from a good red loam to light sand, and on the open banks it is nearly everywhere a fine brown mould, intermixed with limestone. Some of these banks and drier flats on Murrabinna have lately been surveyed, but it has since been determined not to offer the land for sale until the advantages that will result from the drainage have been developed. Indeed, the only land as yet alienated from the Crown within the limits I have described in this and my last chapter is on a portion of the coast ridge extending for some few miles north and south of Kingston, and on the spur of the Mount Benson Range.

Approaching Mount Benson there are some strips of forest land intersecting the course of the Biscuit Flat on an east and west line, and excluding a few patches where there is too much limestone near the surface, and a portion of the lower or coast end of them, which is waterlogged in winter, all this land is decidedly fit for the plough, when cleared. The soil is a good red loam, with limestone below. It is moderately timbered with gum, sheaoak, and honeysuckle, and is quite above the reach of the inundations which periodically submerge the surrounding flats. Beyond this on the southward there is another "arm" of the Biscuit Flat, and then you reach the Mount Benson Range. The Mount itself, the highest point of the chain, is a prominent object, towering like a monument above the humbler hills around it, and its barren sides and rugged peak present a stern contrast to their gentler grassy slopes. Here the soil varies in the most fitful alternations, from almost pure sand and a black or red sandy loam to a chocolate marl, stiffening at places to good honest clay, and still with the limestone subsoil. Except on the highest rises of the range and on patches where the stone

is too thick on the surface, the whole of this belt of undulating country, having an average width of some four miles, and extending from the Mount about six miles to the coast, is good agricultural land. Wattles are very plentiful amongst the timber, and if the present timber licences were somewhat modified wattle bark would become a good export article from Lacepede Bay. Now a payment of £5 annually is required, and it is more than a working man can reasonably afford merely for collecting the bark.

I take it that the Mount Benson Range will be the natural Southern boundary of the local trade of Lacepede Bay. It is almost equi-distant as between Kingston and Robe, and with a port on either side, it is unlikely produce will be carted across the range unnecessarily. The Mount Benson country is held now under two pastoral leases by Mr. Dugald Smith and Mr. Seymour (of Mosquito Plains), but the latter gentleman has taken up at the upset price, after it had passed the hammer, a block of some 4,000 or 5,000 acres of the land I have already described as trending to the coast from the spur of the range. Those who in visiting the district keep only to the beaten highway, would scarcely suspect the existence there of such a large extent of really good land. I came upon it quite unexpectedly in following down the coast line, from Guichen Bay to Cape Jaffa, and was so delighted with the prospect it afforded that I turned off the beach and struck through it back to the range. After riding some two or three miles, I was agreeably surprised to find a genuine farm homestead, and signs of cultivation which fully justified the opinions I had already formed of the capabilities of the soil. But unfortunately the enterprising pioneer of agriculture, who has invaded the hitherto sacred recesses of pastoral monopoly with plough and seed, has only been able to secure one section of 80 acres, nearly all the rest of the alienated land having become, as I have said, the property of Mr. Seymour. I was glad to meet, too, at this farm, an intelligent and hale old gentleman, the father of the owner, who has been better known in the past history of South Australia than he is now. His name, which I am sure he will permit me to mention, is Henry Paddon, and he was an active and useful colonist here when most of us were strangers to South Australia. It was edifying to a degree to listen to the tale he told of the publication of a pamphlet on iron ores, written by himself many years ago, for the authorship of which he avers an honorable member for a northern district has recently received the credit. In connection with this farm, it is interesting to note that Mr. James Paddon, the owner, has this year "mended" a portion of his land with sea-weed, carted from the adjacent beach, at the rate of 12 tons to the acre. The results of the experiment will be worth observing.

There are some other conditions pertaining to the land under notice which must be recorded. Firstly, the "coast disease" is very prevalent and fatal here. I shall, further on in these articles, state all the particulars I have been able to gather respecting this insidious and mysterious malady, but for the present I will merely note that its ravages amongst sheep, horses, and cattle are severe even on the dry soils of Mount Benson, but are still more extensive on the drier chain of sand hills which intervenes between the range and Guichen Bay. Then, secondly, the kangaroo nuisance is acquiring the most astonishing and serious proportions here. The plan chiefly resorted to for the annihilation of the pest

is altogether inefficient for the purpose, and must continue to be so while it is only partially adopted. The occupiers of the two Mount Benson runs, Messrs. Seymour & Smith, pay the blacks in the district 6d. per head for all the kangaroos they kill, and supply them with guns and ammunition. Up to the present time 30,000 head have been paid for at this rate on these two runs alone, and I am assured that a blackfellow has sometimes earned as much as £4 per week in the pursuit. Notwithstanding all this wholesale destruction I scarcely rode 200 yards in any direction about Mount Benson without seeing some of the species, and fresh tracks are everywhere visible. Once I started a mob that could only be counted by thousands, and extended from the extremes of its right and left flanks fully a quarter of a mile. It is computed that two of these animals will consume as much feed as three sheep, and from that some idea may be formed of the extent to which the kangaroo nuisance reduces the actual grazing value of country where they abound. I hope in the interests of our earlier history, our nationality, and field sports, that the marsupial species will never be exterminated in Australia, but unless a means can be devised for giving an actual money value to their flesh, skins, or bones, something will have to be done, if necessary by legislative enactment, to check their further increase. More of this anon.

I have now indicated the nature of all the country within a radius of from 15 to 20 miles of Lacepede Bay. There are two other questions to be dealt with in connection with it before I come to the description of the port itself, and the trade it already possesses, and ought legitimately to command. First, the indigenous products of the district; and secondly, the present results of cultivation there. I am afraid the former will not present a very important or extensive list. The people of Kingston take credit under this head for the Caoutchouc or Cake Petroleum recently discovered in the vicinity of Salt Creek, but whatever value the article may be proved to possess, I scarcely think it will ever become, after the opening of the Coorong, an export from Lacepede Bay, for the water carriage from the Creek to Goolwa will certainly compete with the not very much less distance by land to Kingston. It may, however, be discovered more to the southward of Salt Creek, in which case it would probably go to Kingston for export. Of course every one has seen the samples that were exhibited in Adelaide about a year ago. I believe the source from which the substance exudes upon the surface is not yet known, but it is a singular fact that on some places where the deposit was destroyed by fire last summer the stuff is again covering the ground. I understand that a parcel of it has actually been sold at £12 10s. per ton, and that a recent analysis shows it to contain an oil valuable for machinery, besides kerosine and stearine. I have already mentioned the quantity of wattles at Mount Benson, and with due liberality on the part of Government, wattle bark might be added to the exports of the district. Also, if proper precautions were adopted, it ought surely to be possible to get some value out of the kangaroos, especially when they abound so near a shipping place. Kangaroo skins well tanned make soft and yet durable leather, and kangaroo hams well cured would tempt an impartial epicure to a hearty meal. Even the bones of the animal must have some value, if not for manufacturing purposes, certainly for manure. Only the other day a Lake Hawdon settler

was advertising for a man to kill kangaroos at sixpence a head, and all the employer asks for as evidence of slaughter is "the lugs." I am satisfied that if two or three men took up the trade, who understood thoroughly how to cure a ham and tan a hide, they might make a good profit from those operations, and a good wage from the head-money to boot, besides contributing to a national benefit. Carbonate of magnesia is found at places to the north-west of Lacepede Bay. It is remarkably pure, forming little rises, externally not unlike beehives, and containing within a mass like fine flour in appearance.

Now, as to the results of cultivation. I have already said that the farms in the district are confined at present to the coast ridge, which extends from near Coolatoo to Mount Benson, and to one occupation at the back of the range. On the northern side of the Bay, they commence about eight miles from the township, and the principal farmers are Mr. J. D. Cave, Mr. Oakley, Mr. Smith, Mr. Lane, and the Messrs. J. & A. Cooke. Last year—I am now, of course, depending upon information, and not personal observation—there were grown 350 tons of hay upon 225 acres of land, the yield upon some paddocks exceeding 2½ tons to the acre, and the average of all being more than 1½ tons. Two thousand one hundred bushels of wheat were grown on 139 acres, part of which has been cropped for three years successively. The yield upon some paddocks was as high as 30 bushels to the acre, the average of the whole being 16 bushels. I saw several hundred bushels on the floor of Messrs. Cooke's store, at Kingston, and the grain is large and plump. Other crops have been grown successfully, as, for instance, oats, barley, rye, onions, and mangold wurtzel. I am particular in mentioning these facts, because of an unjust prejudice which has grown up against this end of the district, and because I believe them to afford reasonable evidence of the suitability of the locality for agricultural settlement where the land is fit. That I have sufficiently described in detail, and its area will be immensely increased by the drainage works, which have been already initiated. The farmers—tenant farmers some of them—who have been settled there for several years, do not complain so much of the quality of the soil, or the expense of clearing it, as of the coast disease and the strong winds which sometimes prevail there. In short, to compare the present agricultural resources of the Lacepede Bay District with Mount Gambier, Penola, or even Narracoorte, would be absurd; but because it may suffer by comparison with lands that are exceptionally rich it ought not to be altogether ignored, and I am confident of seeing in the not very distant future an uninterrupted chain of prosperous farming settlements around the township of Kingston.

CHAPTER III.

THE TOWN AND PORT OF LACEPEDE.—ITS PRESENT TRADE AND FUTURE USEFULNESS.

HONEST Gratiano in the fulness of his anger and scorn, culminated his objurgations of defeated Shylock in the wish that he should have godfathers enough to bring him "to the gallows—not the font!" An almost equally severe affliction has been imposed upon luckless Lacepede. Would any one, uninitiated in the mysteries of the christenings of things and places, ever guess without a prompter, that the appellations of Lacepede Bay, Port Lacepede, Port Caroline, Kingston, Maria Creek, The Creek, &c., &c., were all intended to signify the same town and port? Yet it is a fact that such is the case; and the "et ceteras" with which the catalogue is closed are intended as a saving clause if the compilation is incomplete, as judging from indications no doubt it is. I think the interests of the place, and its inhabitants would be promoted if only its original and euphonious name of Lacepede were retained. The multiplicity of titles it possesses now can only create confusion, and will even mislead strangers as to the locality. "Port Lacepede" would be a significant and distinctive name, and for a town that is absolutely a seaport it would be impossible to select a better one.

It must be admitted that beyond a wide expanse of ocean in repose, and the belt of timber which skirts the coast line, there is but little in the appearance of Lacepede—as I shall call it—to gratify an exacting lover of the picturesque in Nature. The town itself is as yet scattered and incongruous. The buildings are dispersed over about a half mile square of ground. What are to be the "streets" of the future are barely defined now. In promenading some of the principal thoroughfares you have to toil over sand ridges. Blackfellows' wurleys, primitive and pungent, stand cheek by jowl with stately edifices of enterprise and refinement. Blear-eyed lubras, costumed with short pipes and scanty blankets, squat in the sunshine, where presently dainty dames in furbelows and feathers will promenade upon verandahed pavements. Dusky, curly pated, snuffling piccanninies, ranging from pure black to octoroon, gambol there unhindered, and all around the pleasant simplicity, quietness, and freedom of the bush prevail. Even many of the white inhabitants are only "housed" in tents, and in some quarters of the town shoes and stockings are not held to be essential to the conditions of civilised life. But with all this there are evidences enough of present prosperity and future progress to arrest the attention of even the casual observer. There are stores with goodly stocks; inns with the significant cluster of saddle-horses at the bridle-posts outside; cheerful-looking cottages with a bit of white paint, and a bright *parterre*; a long range of substantial warehouses, and others in course of erection. The ring of the carpenter's hammer and the clink of the mason's chisel have a meaning in their sound, and it tells the tale of enterprise and progress. Prominent amongst the new buildings approaching completion is the new Telegraph and Post Office. It is a handsome and convenient structure, and the establishment of telegraphic communication which will now soon be afforded will be as welcome as it is a necessary boon to the inhabitants. A large new store is also being built, and a two-storied and commodious hotel, which will be the third in the township. All these buildings are in close proximity to the jetty, but somewhat removed from the portion of the township which is most populated now. Messrs. Cooke's stores and offices are on the beach frontage and flush with the road approaching the jetty.

The harbor is without doubt one of the most remarkable in the world. Apparently a wide open roadstead, exposed to the full swell of the ocean, and terminating in a low shallow beach, it is nevertheless almost without a wave even when, beyond its bounds, old Neptune is roaring and raging in his wildest fury. No one who has ever witnessed the wonderful calmness of its waters when the smartest craft were hardly able to weather the storm outside has withheld his testimony to the security it offers to vessels already there, or as a harbor of refuge to others in distress if they can gain its shelter. Various theories have been propounded as to the cause of its perpetual calmness, but the fact is acknowledged on all hands. Dr. W. J. Browne, who is largely interested in the southern end of the district, when examined before the South-Eastern Improvement Committee of last year, gave the following evidence, which is terse, but explicit and convincing:—" I know Lacepede Bay to be a remarkably safe port. I was out in a very severe gale of wind some years ago, but I think I may say that the Ant (steamer) and the whole of her passengers would have been lost had it not been that she sought refuge in Lacepede Bay. There we found it quite calm, although the sea was in a fearful state outside." Captain Douglas, the President of the Marine Board, when examined before the same Committee, attributed the safety of the bay "to the shelter of the Cape Jaffa reef, which intercepts the ocean swell, and to the gradual shoaling of the water to the shore." But Mr. Goyder, the Surveyor-

General, who has personally taken soundings for seven miles from the shore purposely to ascertain the cause of the remarkable stillness which prevails, gives an explanation which certainly appears more complete and feasible. The reef to which Captain Douglas refers no doubt assists in the protection of the bay on the south-west side, but it does not enclose the roadstead. Mr. Goyder says the bottom of the bay presents a series of natural breakwaters. There are sudden and precipitous falls for from eight to twenty feet from one level to another, and the incoming swell breaking upon these successive walls is perpetually thrown back to meet and break the force of its follower, until, as the motion of the wave extends itself to the comparatively shallow waters where vessels are moored, its power is expended, and it finally washes but feebly on the shore. I cannot doubt the correctness of Mr. Goyder's premises, and that being conceded, his conclusion seems natural and convincing. From the survey of the Bay, I gather that its total area of comparatively smooth water is 78 square miles without a known rock. It contains 44 square miles, with a depth of from 30 to 60 feet; 23 square miles, with a depth of from 15 to 30 feet; and 11 square miles, having a depth of less than 15 feet. The present jetty only goes into some seven or eight feet of water, but it is said there is a depth of 24 feet within three-quarters of a mile from the shore. It will undoubtedly be necessary, in order to provide for the future trade of the port, to extend the jetty to deeper water, but I will reserve this point for the present. I am quite aware of the delicate ground I shall be getting on when I come to discuss the requirements of rival ports, and I shall complete first of all my descriptive notes of the whole district.

Some particulars of the trade which has been hitherto developed at Lacepede will be interesting. The port has only been established some six years, and the shipment of wool there was not commenced on at all a large scale until the season of 1865-6. In that year the exports of wool amounted to a total of 1,064 bales, of which 287 bales were from the Northern sheep shorn in the South-East in consequence of the drought, and 777 bales, the produce of the district proper. In 1866-7 the export reached 1,391 bales, all the produce of the district, or nearly double the amount of local-grown wool shipped in the previous year. In the ensuing season, with even existing facilities, there will be, 1 venture to predict, a considerable increase upon this quantity, and it is not improbable the shipments will reach 2,500 to 3,000 bales. A statement has been handed to me by which it appears that there are 30 sheep stations in South Australia, yielding 5,500 bales, and about 15 in Victoria, yielding 2,500 bales, which are nearer to Port Lacepede than to any other shipping place. I cannot vouch for the accuracy of this computation myself, but I know that it comes from a trustworthy source, and its correctness is purely a question of fact. Assuming it to be correct, it does not follow, however, that this total of 8,000 bales will be immediately shipped at Lacepede, or that all the stations producing it will at once draw their supplies from thence. There are various interests at work which have an entirely opposite tendency at present, but they must inevitably either assume a new aspect or die out in the future. Lacepede Bay is so good a harbor, and facilities for shipment there may be so easily rendered unexceptionable, that it must become in the common order of things the outlet for all the country to which it is absolutely nearer than any other port, if even it does not command a more distant trade, excepting only where—as in the case of the Coorong—the cheapness of water carriage may compete with a shorter distance of land traffic. It is certain, therefore, that the trade of the port will be progressive for years to come, and in recognising its value and importance as the best fitting and most easily turned key to a certain extent of country, which—when present prejudices have run their course—will be determined partly by the lines upon the map, but chiefly by the natural features of the country itself, I am committing myself to nothing that ought to excite the jealousy or opposition of settlers beyond those limits. At the same time I do not overlook the fact that where, as at Mount Gambier and Penola, population is so much larger, settlement so much more advanced, and even undeveloped resources are richer, the necessity for the supply of facilities for traffic and shipment, if they do not exist naturally, is more urgent and immediate. I say this parenthetically, lest the people at the southern end of the district should imagine that, because I have not allowed myself to be biassed by the prevailing antipathy to its Northern port, I shall also run counter to popular opinion by underrating their claims. And now "to return to our muttons." An exact estimate of the past and present inward trade of Port Lacepede may be formed from the tonnage of the goods landed there by the two vessels regularly engaged in the local traffic. In 1864 and part of 1865, the imports were 410 tons all by the Swallow (cutter). In 1865-6 they were 528 tons by the Swallow, and 130 tons by the Kangaroo (schooner), while for 1866-7, they have already reached 760 tons by the Swallow, and 190 tons by the Kangaroo. These imports consist of

general merchandise, and as they all come from Port Adelaide, and are mostly duty paid there, they do not figure in the Customs returns of Lacepede. The figures have been obtained from the manifests of the two vessels, and have been obligingly given to me by Messrs. J. and A. Cooke. Some of these imports have already been sent by dray to Border Town and Narracoorte, and even over the Border into Victoria. When I was at the port, I saw two heavily laden drays leave Messrs. Cooke's store, and a few days later, when en route to the Tatiara, I overtook them within a few miles of their destination at Border Town. It is a fact, therefore, that some residents in the Tatiara have discovered that Lacepede is the nearest and cheapest port for them, and that the foundation of what must eventually become an extensive trade is already laid.

There is one want at Lacepede to which, as it has no bearing whatever on the interests of the district as a whole, I may as well advert at once. It is the necessity for the establishment of a Local Court there. At present, in whatever litigation the people of Lacepede may be involved, they must attend the Court at Guichen Bay, and it of course frequently happens that the expenses of the journey, and the loss of time it necessitates, amount to far more than the sum at issue. A few weeks ago 19 summonses were issued against people at Lacepede by the Crown Lands Ranger for illegally depasturing cattle, and although in some cases there were absolute bars to action, the journey to Robe became a necessity to the defendants. There is a great hardship in this which the Government might easily remedy. Mr. Gower, the Resident Stipendiary Magistrate, at Robe has only the Court at that place to attend, and it would not be unreason-

c

able to ask him to ask him to take duty once a month at Kingston. For the present accommodation might be found for the sittings of the Court without the necessity of building a Court-House ; and all that would be necessary would be to "proclaim" some place in due form, make the arrangement with Mr. Gower, and appoint a local resident to act as Clerk of the Court, for which, as the duties would be light at present, a nominal salary would suffice. Considering that now there is no Court held between Wellington and Guichen Bay, the reasonableness of the claim which the people of Lacepede Bay and the vicinity have in this matter will, I am sure, be acknowledged. Another inconvenience, which also might be easily remedied, results from there being only one resident Justice of the Peace at Lacepede Bay. There are, of course, other "requirements" there, but as they in a measure affect other parts of the district also, I shall, in accordance with my plan, reserve their consideration for the present.

CHAPTER IV.

FROM MOUNT BENSON TO GUICHEN BAY.—THE COAST DISEASE.—THE TOWN OF ROBE.—THE ADJACENT COUNTRY AND THE LAKES.

FROM the Mount Benson range — the natural barrier from which the stream of commerce must flow to Port Lacepede in one direction and to Port Robe in the other—the track to Guichen Bay, or Robe, lies on an almost due south line. There is one large teatree swamp just beyond Mr. Seymour's station, and a road has been embanked through the worst part of it. Then you enter a long, weary chain of sand hummocks, which extend, without a break, almost to Robe. To the eastward the Stone Hut range, heading the Biscuit Flat, trends to and beyond Lake Hawdon, and, except near the Lake, there is very little country available for agriculture. The coast disease is very prevalent, and even more than usually severe on these sand hummocks, and the comparative scarcity of kangaroos there is attributed to the sagacity of those animals in avoiding the most infected localities. As I have just now mentioned the Biscuit Flat, I will supply an omission here by explaining a peculiarity from which it takes its name. Over its whole extent it is thickly covered with flat round incrustations of limestone with small indentations upon their upper surface, giving them a singularly close resemblance to genuine biscuits, which is rather increased than otherwise by the fact that their size varies from that of the diminutive "Picnic," to the substantial "Abernethy." The Rev. J. E. Tenison Woods in his valuable and interesting "geological observations" of the district, gives a very feasible explanation of their origin. Alluding to the fact that the surface of these wet flats is generally pitted over with little depressions in which the remaining water collects when the dry weather sets in, and that they are the last to dry up, he remarks that in doing so, a small quantity of lime and pipeclay (in which soil they only occur) gets hardened into a cake, and these cakes becoming afterwards detached from the soil derive their singular but uniform appearance from the action of rain and atmospheric influences. Mr. Woods is evidently confident that this is the true explanation of the "biscuits," and with all the enthusiasm of a geologist he adds :—" How · simply they tell their own story when examined ; so true it is that natural phenomena are open before us like a book to read from if we will only pay attention to every word and letter."

Then as to the "coast disease." The hummocks I have mentioned are certainly infected as severely, or probably more severely, than any other part of the district. What is the real cause of the plague, or why it appears in certain localities where widely different conditions prevail, and does not touch others where there is apparently precisely the same character of soil, climate, and vegetation, I am quite unable to explain. Theories enough to bewilder the most painstaking and discriminating enquirer have been propounded, but I have heard none as yet which stated experiences will not in some degree refute. Noxious gases exhaling from stagnant water is given, for instance, as one theory of cause ; but then these very sandhills, fatally pregnant with the disease, but quite dry and above and away from all stagnant waters, confound such a supposition on the face of it. The disease prevails too on the dry warm ridge extending from near Coolatoo to Mount Benson, and through the Mount Benson and Stone Hut Ranges. Other theorists ascribe the cause to a poison plant as yet undetected, while others again maintain that any vegetation produced in certain localities will impart the poison. Some say that horses infected with the disease, and fed upon hay grown where it prevails, will die, but that if fed upon imported fodder they will recover. But here again experience will supply exceptions enough to destroy the rule. It must not be forgotten either that the disease is not peculiar to the South-East. I have heard of it on Yorke's Peninsula and at Port Lincoln, and also on the coast of the Western District of Victoria, and even beyond Port Phillip Heads. In the South-East it appears to be chiefly confined to the country at the head of the Coorong, from whence it extends to Lake George on the south, and variously, to Penola on the east. One fact which is quite beyond cavil is important—the disease invariably assumes its severest form on the dry lands from about August to November, or in the spring season, when the feed grows quickly after the rains, especially on the light warm sandy soils, but is comparatively washy and innutritious. This, I think, rather favors the theory which not a few maintain, that after all, the origin of the whole thing is in the poverty of the feed at certain times and places. But at any rate something ought to be done to prove the bane, in order that the antidote may be supplied. The disease renders a large tract of country comparatively valueless, at all events for grazing purposes, and the cost of detecting its origin—and surely that is not impossible—would be money well expended in the interest of the community generally. Even a careful compilation of all the facts which actual experience will afford would be useful, if only as indicating the direction enquiry, to be assisted by practical tests, should take. For instance, Mr. Edward Stockdale, one of the oldest settlers in the South-East, told me that on the Stone Hut Range—appropriately named from the outcroppings of limestone— the disease is fatal to sheep, but scarcely affects horses or cattle, while on the adjacent flats, it tells more severely upon cattle than horses, and the fatter the beasts the more aggravated is the disease. There must be a reason for all these circumstances, and practice and science combined should solve the mystery. The Legislature has already evinced a sense of its responsibilities as to diseases in wheat, and it is certainly desirable that provision should also be made for discovering the cause of coast disease.

There is one hotel on the road from Mount Benson to Robe, and after leaving it the next indications of settlement are at Newton, a "suburb" of Guichen Bay, the intervening distance being about 12 miles. At Newton the bush track through the sand hummocks strikes the main line of road to Penola, which at that point and for a few miles further on the line is metalled to Robe. The scenery too improves materially. The coast ridge on the right of the road is bolder and richer in vegetation than the hummocks you have left ; cottage or villa residences with trim fences and gay garden nooks are dotted here and there, and on the left there are several broad lagoons, shallow, but pretty notwithstanding. Wild fowl may be seen even now lazily lounging on those lazy

waters, but a fellmongery establishment there proves that enterprise may apply them to a more useful if less romantic purpose. Another mile and you are within the precincts of Robe proper. Imagine, if you please, a long length of road bordered at first by paddocks, then cottages and gardens, then stray shops and miscellaneous buildings until you get in the very thick of bakers, butchers, bootmakers, tailors, saddlers, chemists, public-houses, multum in parvo stores, then other actual streets branching from this main road, and finally, dignified and withal handsome banking-houses fronting an open space, which, I suppose, is intended to become an ornamental square or crescent in the future. To the left there is rising ground, with a church and some other buildings dotted about. To the right the calm waters of the Bay, with probably a steamer or one or two vessels at anchor ; before you another hotel, and beyond it again capacious stores and goodly habitations. Indeed, I was astonished to find how in seven years, which had elapsed since I was last there, the town had increased, not only in extent, but in the various accommodations it affords. The place is still essentially a wool and pastoral port, and all the export and most of the import trade passes through the hands of Messrs. George Ormerod & Co. I am certainly doubtful whether it is destined in the future to retain all the trade it possesses now, because that must necessarily be affected by the development of Lacepede Bay, on the north, as its commercial relations have already been by the opening of MacDonnell Bay on the south. · But before going fully into this question, I will complete my notes of the adjacent country.

One especial feature of the neighborhood is the chain of lakes, which extends from Lake Hawdon on the north to Lake Bonney on the south. The several lakes are separated from each other in nearly every case by narrow strips of land, and it is the opinion of most scientific men who have seen them that they are now drying up with comparative rapidity, and that not very many years ago they formed one long narrow body of water, resembling pretty nearly what the Coorong is now. Besides the more important of these lakes, which comprise Lakes Hawdon, Eliza, St. Clair, George, and Bonney, there are a large number of smaller ones, varying in area from about five to fifty acres, which add largely to the romantic beauty of the scenery. Indeed, in this last respect Guichen Bay excels every other part of the South-Eastern District, unless it be Mount Gambier itself, but there nature has presented her loveliness under quite a different aspect. The rugged precipitous walls of extinct craters, and the supernatural stillness and depth of the waters that have replaced volcanic fires, impress the beholder with wonder and awe. But around Guichen Bay the scenery is beautiful in its simplicity, and yet perfect in its loveliness. Take, for example, the immediate vicinity of Lake Eliza. The road thither from Robe lies through a pleasant jumble of hills, lightly timbered, and having in places a light loamy soil, but with a good deal of downright sand intersecting the better strips. Then you cross some open plains, subject to inundation in very wet seasons, and enclosed by perpetually recurring belts of gum and sheaoak where the ground is elevated slightly above the level which the water reaches. You are running a south-east line now, and have the coast ridge of sand hills on your right. Ascend one of the highest of these eminences and you have a view

which not even the Lake of Como, as word-painted by Bulwer's florid pen, can excel. At your feet are the broad glittering waters of Lake Eliza, encircled with the shrublike tea-tree, the dingier honeysuckle, or the graceful sheaoak. Grassy plains (we may forget now they will presently be swamps), divided by long lines of timber fill up the space to the sandhills, and there, embossomed in those undulating settings which the geniality of the season has clothed in the gayest verdure of spring, you have a wealth of beauty in the smaller lakes that—brightest and most brilliant of all—are flashing in the sunshine like diamonds in an emerald wreath. For the outside border of all this matchless scene you have the ocean itself, and its dull roar upon the beach below you can but suggest the thought, are geologists really true theorists when they affirm that in a former age those waves rolled over the intervening glories of hill, lake, and plain we are admiring now, to yonder range which forms the opposite framework of the picture? And if so, will the changes of future cycles beat back old ocean further still, and wrest from his grasp another landscape so rich in loveliness? There are certainly phenomena enough to suggest all manner of speculative thought. Every tree that you pass that has been blown down and is lying now with its roots exposed, reveals clinging to those roots, or embedded in the soil where once they grew, innumerable oyster shells, many of them being in a perfect state of preservation. Mr. Woods would probably exclaim of these as he did of the stone biscuits, "How simply they tell their own story when examined;" but the evidence, however simple, is impressive and profound.

Another of the phenomena peculiar to the South-Eastern District is very prominent here, and it will be best understood by the term "underground drainage." But by this something more is inferred than the mere percolation of surface water to a lower level through a porous soil. It is assumed that there are actually underground rivers which absorb and carry off a great deal of the swamp water of the interior, receiving it through what are called the "runaway holes" that abound on all the swampy ground. These remarks will apply with even greater force to the country more to the southward, but there are some who maintain that Lake Hawdon and Lake Eliza might be effectually drained by boring holes to these subterranean water channels. Instances are freely given in which evidences of the existence of these underground streams have been obtained in sinking wells. It is a singular fact, too, that of the chain of lakes I have described the water of some is quite fresh and of others salt or brackish. Lake Eliza, for instance, is salt, while Lake George is fresh. They are not, therefore, all maintained by the drainage of the super-abundant rainfall on the higher levels, although apparently they originally formed one united stream.

When I was on this country a survey was going on near Lake Eliza. Some of the land pegged out is good open forest plain, having a light red loam and plenty of limestone. The lines all terminate at the sand hills but run through a good deal of swampy ground to near the margin of the lake. Much of the wet land there, however, is rich in quality, and may be easily drained into the Lake by ordinary races. Mr. Denning, an enterprising and practical farmer, is cultivating with remarkable success a strip of alluvial soil which he has drained in this way entirely at his own expense and risk. There is about 18 inches of black mould on a light sandy subsoil. The drains, which are 10 feet wide and average about five feet in depth, have laid this land quite dry, and potatoes and mangolds grow well there. This is one practical instance of what may be done by the drainage of these rich flats. Indeed time appears to be silently working a beneficial change, for the oldest settlers assure me that less ground is covered with water there than was formerly the case, and on the Lake Hawdon run good grass is obtained where 20 years ago there was only a wild waste of swamp and morass. This is attributed to an absolute change in the seasons, or in the features of the country itself, although it is admitted that during the last year or two, the Narrow Neck cutting has relieved this particular locality of a good deal of the water which used to find its way there from the Mount Muirhead flat. Fifteen years ago, a man named Sharp was drowned on what is now the main road from the Stone Hut Range to Mr. Stockdale's station. For some years past, there has been no water on that portion of the flat at all, and intermingled with the large dead timber, evidently killed by former floods, are healthy vigorous trees of recent growth.

Beyond the chain of lakes there is not much good land in the Guichen Bay district towards either Penola, on which line swamp, heath, and scrub prevail, or towards Mount Muirhead, except in narrow strips or patches. There is, however, some rich black soil about the racecourse, some four miles from Robe, on which excellent results have been obtained, both in gardening and farming, and a number of good sections may be selected from the Lake Eliza survey, which will soon I presume, be advertised for sale. Hitherto the locality has not grown produce enough for its own consumption—of hay at all events—but this ought not to be the case. There is enough agricultural land, although not in very large blocks, to warrant cultivation on a sufficient scale for home use, if not for export ; and if the scheme of draining Lake Hawdon and Lake Eliza results successfully, a rich field of industry will be opened here as in other portions of the South-East.

CHAPTER V.

THE TOWN AND PORT OF ROBE.—ITS TRADE AND INSTITUTIONS.—WOOL FREIGHTS,

ADELAIDE V. MELBOURNE.—PASTORAL TENURES AND IMPROVEMENTS ON RUNS.

ROBE, as I have said, is essentially a pastoral port. That is to say, its export of wool constitutes its whole outward trade, while its imports consist for the most part of station stores. What else is imported there is confined to the requirements of the inhabitants of the town itself, and they, directly or indirectly, minister to station wants. Messrs. Geo. Ormerod & Co. are, it may be said, the commercial representatives of the place, for I suppose every bale of wool which is shipped there passes through their hands. The port was opened in 1854 or 1855, and for a considerable period since then it remained THE port of the South-East, having only to contend with Portland Bay on the Victorian side. The opening of MacDonnell Bay, some six or seven years ago, deprived it at once of the proportion of the Mount Gambier trade which it had obtained, and now it is threatened with a further curtailment of its commerce by the development of Lacepede Bay on the North. Mr. Ormerod has, however, during a long series of years, commanded so thoroughly the confidence and respect of the South-Eastern settlers, that while his connection with the port—which he may be fairly said to have founded and nurtured —lasts, it is not likely to lose, in any material degree, the trade it has retained till now. I could name several settlers who send their wool 10, 15, or even 20 miles further than is now necessary, in order to ship through the old house, and they will continue to do so until the name of Ormerod is taken down at Robe, or put up elsewhere. When either of these contingencies occur a good deal of the present trade of Robe will, inevitably, be lost to it, but it is not too much to hope that that will be fully replaced by the increase of settlement and the development of new enterprises in the immediate district. I have already indicated what the agricultural resources of the locality are, and the people of the town will certainly have nothing to deplore if whatever decrease may be sustained in the shipments of wool is counterbalanced by the increasing export of farm produce.

Of course the material feature of Robe is its harbor, and the facilities for shipment. Guichen Bay, as the harbor is called, is formed by a deep indentation on the coast line south-east of Cape Jaffa. If is five miles by three in extent, and is landlocked on all points except from north-west to west. The holding ground is good, and it is fortunate the prevailing winds during the summer, or wool season, are from the south and south-east. The present shipping accommodation—I allude only to the loading and discharge of vessels—is miserably inadequate to the trade that has been done there. The old jetty, which is 300 feet in length, only goes into shallow water, and even coasting steamers are unable to go alongside. This, however, is being remedied, for the new jetty now in course of erection will go into 14 feet at low-water springs. Its total length will be 1,022 feet. At 600 feet it curves from a straight line to face north-west, and at 840 feet it opens to a double width, terminating in an L head. It is close planked, and there will be a single line of rails to the extension in width, and then a double line. A receiving-shed is to be erected on the beach, but the Governmental finger is clearly apparent in the arrangements respecting it. For some inscrutable reason, which I can only describe as the dregs of a tiff between the Marine Board and the Public Works Office, the jetty is carried out flush with the lifeboat-shed recently erected at a cost of some £200 or £300, and which has now to be pulled down in conse-

quence. The jetty might have been equally well placed, a little on one side of this point, and in that case a better approach could also have been obtained direct from the Flagstaff. Now, not only will a good deal of cutting be required to make the approach, but it will be far less convenient, and as for the boat-shed, it must go. The receiving-shed, which is included in the vote of £7,000 for the jetty, is to be 40 feet by 25 in the clear. When all these works are completed the facilities of the port will be largely increased, and there will be little else to ask for in that respect. The Penola, which trades regularly to Robe, will, under favorable circumstances, be able to come alongside the new jetty, and one special advantage to the district, and let us hope to Adelaide, will be the accommodation that will be afforded for the shipment of fat stock for the metropolitan market. Mr. Bailey, of Melbourne, is the contractor for the new jetty, and excepting only some unavoidable delay in obtaining the timber from Swan River, he has made good progress with the work.

Some years ago Mr. Ormerod shipped wool direct from Robe to London, but he has now altogether abandoned that practice, and all his consignments, unless specially ordered for Adelaide, go to Melbourne for shipment in the London clippers. As his experience on this point is the key to a question of vital importance to Adelaide interests, I may fairly occupy a few lines on the subject. Adelaide has still to compete with Melbourne for a large proportion of the trade of the South-East. The absurd protective duties of Victoria are, of course, in our favor as to the import trade, but so long as Melbourne wool freights bear the same proportion to Adelaide rates that they do at present we have a most unequal struggle to maintain for the outward trade. Shipment from local ports direct is, no doubt, the most desirable object to be attained in the interest of the producer and the locality, but failing this the advantages of attracting our exports to our own principal port rather than seeing them regularly drafted off to Melbourne, are plainly apparent. As to the first point Mr. Ormerod has abandoned direct shipments to London because he finds he can place his wool in the London market more cheaply and expeditiously by sending it by steamer to Hobson's Bay, and thence to London in the clippers trading between those ports. He holds, too, that even with the increased settlement of the district, and the development of its resources it will still be cheaper to ship via Melbourne than direct to London. In 1865 the freights from Melbourne on his whole shipment of 7,676 bales was only ¼d. per lb., the Adelaide rates at the same time being only a fraction less than a penny per lb. In 1866 the Melbourne rates ranged from ⅜d. to ½d., while from Port Adelaide they averaged ⅝d. Then, besides this, there is the material advantage of quicker dispatch from Melbourne, owing, of course to the greater number of vessels sailing thence. These are unpalatable facts for South Australians ; but the more clearly they are understood the better will be the chance of improving our position in the matter. As it is the fact that almost the whole of the wool produce of the South-east shipped at Robe goes to Melbourne for export, will account in a large measure for the Victorian tendencies of the district, which are nowhere more strongly exemplified than at Robe. Another reason that is given for the preference for Melbourne freights, viz., that the wool is classed as "Port Phillip," and thereby obtains a better reputation in the London market,

I attach but little importance to, for surely wool buyers at home look beyond the mere verbal description of the article. But it is certain, nevertheless, that before South Australia can thoroughly compete with Victoria for the South-Eastern trade she must offer something like equal terms on freights to London. It will be interesting in connection with this subject to state what the wool shipments from Robe have been during the last ten years. In

1856-7 the export was		3,584 bales
1857-8	"	3,298 "
1858-9	"	4,004 "
1859-60	"	5,617 "
1860-61	"	6,452 "
1861-2	"	7,032 "
1862-3	"	7,176 "
1863-4	"	6,950 "
1864-5	"	7,676 "
1865-6	"	7,667 "

and for 1866-7 it reached 8,100 bales. This embraces most of the clips from Mosquito Plains and the intervening country, and from stations in Victoria. The proportion of Victorian wool included will be shown by the subjoined table of comparative values :—

EXPORTS OF WOOL FROM PORT ROBE TO LONDON, FROM JANUARY, 1856, TO DECEMBER 31, 1865.

Years.	Produce of S. Australia.	Produce of Victoria.	Total Export Value.
1856 ...	£36,810	£1,400	£38,210
1857 ...	91,045	21,770	112,815
1858 ...	59,750	15,500	75,250
1859 ...	80,916	12,200	93,116
1860 ...	88,768	39,586	128,354
1861 ...	46,200	23,280	69,480
1862 ...	113,175	37,720	150,895
1863 ...	77,760	33,274	111,034
1864 ...	115,700	38,640	154,340
1865 ...	127,760	35,446	163,206
	£837,884	£258,816	£1,096,700

During these same ten years the total value of wool shipped, via Adelaide, was £80,240, as against £1,096,700 shipped either direct or by way of Melbourne, bringing the total export of Robe to

£1,176,940. The above figures show also that the actual exports of Robe have not decreased since the opening of MacDonnell Bay, but several clips have ceased to be sent there nevertheless. For instance, the Mount Schanck wool, which formerly went to Robe, now naturally goes to MacDonnell Bay; but the increased production on the stations which still adhere to Robe, resulting chiefly from the fencing, will explain what would otherwise appear contradictory.

The import trade of Robe, although it has decreased in the aggregate from two separate causes, presents one welcome feature, in the better position which Adelaide has assumed in respect of it. The decrease is attributable partly, of course, to the opening of MacDonnell Bay, and partly to the improvements on the runs being stopped pending the settlement of the question of future tenure. But, although formerly the balance of that branch of the trade was also in favor of Melbourne, now the proportion, as nearly as can be ascertained, is three-fourths to Adelaide as against one-fourth to Melbourne. This will also explain in a great measure the falling off in the Customs Revenue of Robe, the duties formerly collected there on Melbourne goods being now for the most part paid at Port Adelaide, and the balance of the decrease on that item must be credited to the general reduction of imports consequent upon the employment of less labor on the runs since they have been fenced, and the stoppage of other improvements there, to which I have already adverted. And with reference to this latter point, it is only fair to state that a very strong opinion prevails in the "pastoral" sections of the district, as to the impolicy of leaving the question of the future tenure of the runs in its present uncertain state. No doubt improvements are either stopped altogether or effected in the slightest and most temporary manner pending an understanding being arrived at; and this is not only limiting the productive power of the district, but causing a general stagnation in trade, and crippling the demand for labor. What the lessees ask for is a definite understanding as to the terms upon which the future occupation of the runs may be obtained, and as the old leases with the five years' renewal will run out in 1870, this is manifestly desirable. It is, at all events, certain that until it is arrived at very little will be done for the further improvement of station properties in the South-East.

My notes of Robe would be altogether incomplete without a few descriptive words of the public institutions of that isolated, but pleasant township. There is, perhaps, no other town in the colony so much severed from the possibility of intercourse, except by seaboard, with other centres of population, and yet I am sure there is none more complete within itself in the advantages which result from the development of public enterprise and liberality, and social good fellowship. I am not given, in my scribblings for the press, to trench upon matters affecting Church or Chapel, but Robe possesses such a good and singular claim to notice under this head, that I cannot refrain from alluding to what really affords an apt illustration of the unison and harmony of its people. The population of the place numbers some 500 all told, and it is manifest that so limited a community could not support as many "churches" of varying denominations as there are differing opinions held. Some time ago an attempt was made to establish another ministry there—I am not sure of which denomination—but it has been abandoned, and now the people of all sects unite in supporting *one* place of worship ;* and never was there a better illustration of the axiom that union is strength. The ministration is most efficiently represented, means are plentiful, congregations large, and all the prospects of the Church prosperous and pleasing. There are many places in the world which might imitate the good example of Robe with great advantage. The church—St. Peter's —is situated on an eminence almost in the centre of the township. It is substantially built, and contains 120 sittings. Schools are established in conjunction with it, and there is already a necessity for an extension of accommodation. Another useful institution at Robe is the Literary Institute. The Library already contains 950 volumes, which have been selected with good discrimination. A reading-room, well supplied with current magazine and newspaper literature—the latter, it must be admitted, chiefly Victorian—has been provided, and a piano has been added to the advantages of the institution. There are now 40 subscribers, and as a grant of land has been obtained it is intended to erect a thoroughly suitable building before long.

I have already mentioned the open triangular space near the centre of the township, which is flanked by the handsome offices of the South Australian and National Banks, and a row of shops on the one side, by the Bay on the other, and by the Robe Hotel on its base. Passing beyond this towards the obelisk there are the capacious stores and offices of Messrs. Ormerod & Co., the Custom-House, and a cluster of less important buildings, all overlooking the bay. And behind all these, in what may be almost termed the back slums of the town, are to be found—not without some difficulty —the hovel which does poor duty for a Police-Station, and the miserably inadequate building in which local litigation is decided, and where the periodical gathering of all the dignitaries associated with Supreme Court jurisdiction brings out the improprieties of the premises in forcible relief. You approach this unparalleled hall of justice through a plot of ground on which rank weeds thrive apace. A verandah is generously accepted as a waiting-room for witnesses, clients, prosecutors, or such other persons as may have business there. Then at a step you are in the presence — when the circumambulating Circuit Court, as Mr. Coglin would call it, is sitting—of a full-wigged Judge, and robed Masters, Associates, Advocates, and Tipstaffs ; or, as to the latter, if not, why not ? The dimensions of the apartment where all these dignitaries crowd together are 25 feet by 16, and the ceiling is very near the Judge's wig when he has elbowed his way to the seat reserved for him. There is only one other room in the building, and this the Local Magistrate and Clerk have in daily and joint use. Even the Court, as it is called, has frequently to be lit artificially when there is plenty of daylight outside, and if ever the expedient of ordering witnesses out of Court is resorted to they must needs go *out* in the fullest meaning of the term. To continue to transact the business of either a Local or Circuit Court in such a place is simply an outrage upon decency, and there ought to be no further delay in providing the accommodation which is really so urgently required. A much better, and more convenient site for the new Court-House, which will certainly

---

* Since these remarks were written an attempt has been made to establish a "Bible Christian" Ministry at Robe, and it ought also to be stated that a Roman Catholic priest makes periodical visits to the district.

have to be erected, would be on the Government Reserve, and the present building might be fairly given for the purposes either of a public school or the Institute pending, at all events, the supply of better accommodation.

The Police-Station is, if possible more inadequate, and more wretched in its inconveniences than the so-called Court-House. It is simply a hovel, and consists of one poor apartment, which is used as a trooper's messroom, rooms for two troopers, and two cells, which are unhealthy and unsafe. They are small, low, ill-ventilated and unsound; the timbers are rotting, and the walls and ceiling are barely weatherproof. The place is used also as an aborigines' store. Supplies of tea, sugar, flour, blankets, fishing lines, hooks, pannicans, and other things are kept there, and are issued to the blacks by the police. Dr. Goldsmith, the resident medical officer at Robe, gives also his professional services when they are required. Some time ago it was proposed to appoint a Sub-Protector of Aborigines for the South-East, but I cannot help thinking that a much more satisfactory plan would be to impose upon the various medical officers in the district the responsibility of caring for the physical infirmities and actual wants of the blacks in their immediate locality. It is hardly reasonable to entrust these duties, and the issuing of stores, entirely to the police-trooper who may happen to be in charge of the station; and, on the other hand, no Sub-Protector could deal efficiently with the requirements of so large a district. The Government have already a resident medical officer in each of the principal centres of population, and a small addition to the official emoluments of these gentlemen would no doubt induce them to extend their protection and care to the aborigines who yet remain.

No one, I am sure, who has visited Robe could regret leaving the Court-House, or Police-Station, for a walk to the rising ground, on which the obelisk is placed, and beyond which stands the Gaol. From the obelisk a most interesting view is obtained. The Bay is seen, perhaps, to its greatest advantage, and the lively appearance of the various buildings of the township, enhanced, as it is, by the cheerful color of the stone, and the gentle undulations of the site on which the town stands, make up a very pleasing picture. But we have yet the Gaol to visit, and it is certainly one of the features of Robe. It is a fine substantial stone building, having a massive appearance, and standing in bold relief, upon the summit of a low hill about half a mile south-west of the township. The walls are 15 feet high, and it contains four strong cellars besides turnkeys' apartments, a courtyard, and a large quadrangle. The outer walls of all the cellars are plated with iron, evidently on the principle of locking the stable door when the horse is stolen. Some years ago an enterprising prisoner escaped by knocking a hole in the stone wall, and therefore the iron plating was provided. But at the Mount Gambier Gaol, where no one has as yet bored through the wall, the opportunity for the performance being repeated there is most jealously retained. The only prison inmates of the Gaol at Robe when I visited it were six strapping-looking blackfellows, who had been sentenced to three months' imprisonment with hard labor for breaking into a public-house at Lacepede Bay and drinking feloniously obtained beer. Their sable highnesses looked very lazy and vastly comfortable. They were well clad in prison uniform, and were quite jubilant in assuring me they had "plenty tucker." Their "hard labor" consisted of chopping wood for the turnkey's parlor fire, and sitting still, with the opportunity of soothing their nerves by consuming the gaol ration of tobacco. In plain truth, I can see but little use in maintaining the Gaol at Robe at all. Mount Gambier is the metropolis of the South-East, there is a Gaol there, and to it any prisoners for trial might be sent, at less expense, and with less trouble than they can be housed and guarded at Robe, at the cost of maintaining a separate establishment for the purpose. There are several respects in which the Robe Gaol is insufficiently supplied. There ought, for instance, to be separate cells, and a separate yard for female prisoners, and it is scarcely prudent to leave the whole establishment, however many or whatever prisoners may be there, in the charge of one man. He would necessarily be in a large measure at the mercy of any gang of desperadoes determined to strike for freedom and revenge ; and yet it seems unreasonable to increase the cost of an establishment which is fortunately so little used. It would be better far to do away with the Gaol establishment altogether, and concentrate some further expenditure and improvements upon the kindred institution at Mount Gambier. More than this, the Robe Gaol would make an excellent Police-Station, which, as I have shown, is so urgently needed there.

As the Chairman of the South-Eastern Road Board is a Robe man, I may appropriately allude to the constitution of that Board before concluding my say about the township. Mr. Ormerod is the Chairman, and the other members are Messrs. Fidler and Crouch, of Mount Gambier, Mr. C. MacKenzie, of Penola, and Mr. Adam Smith, of Mosquito Plains. Thus it will be seen the Lacepede Bay end of the district is entirely unrepresented, and this is an oversight which ought to be adjusted in any future appointments. The Board has expended £35,000 since its establishment in May, 1866, and the beneficial results of its works are plainly apparent in different parts of the district. About five miles of the main line from Robe to Penola have been metalled, and 20 miles have been formed over the Stone Hut-road. Contracts are in progress for clearing the remainder of the distance, and this will be a considerable boon to the settlers along the line whose business relations are with Robe.

CHAPTER VI.

From Reedy Creek to Narracoorte.—The Mosquito Plains.—By Morambra and Padthaway to Tatiara.

Eastward of Lacepede Bay, I have described the country as far as the Reedy Creek Range, and I will now resume my work at that point. What I have already said of the country between the Maria Creek Swamp and Reedy Creek, viz., that it varies with extreme regularity from wet flats and teatree swamps to scrubby rises, more or less stony, with occasional banks of dry light soil, will apply also for some distance further eastward. The Avenue Flats lie beyond the Reedy Creek Range, and run in parallel lines with it for its whole length. The soil upon them is of the same description as nearer Lacepede Bay, but not so rich as either the Maria Creek Swamp or the swamp soils of the southern end of the district. In places too the limestone is very near the surface, and the present vegetation is coarse and innutritious. On Hensley's station, which is nearly equi-distant between Kingston and Narracoorte, there are a series of fine open banks of dry chocolate loam and limestone encircling patches of swampy ground. Further on, the country degenerates again, until at Mount Misery—aptly enough named—you reach the very acme of sterility and desolation. There the soil, if it can be called so, is for the most part sandstone or limestone ; in fact it is stony altogether, and from the summit of the Mount, which I took some pains to ascend, you look out upon a barren hopeless prospect of sand ridges, and scrub, and stone, varied only by the stretches of swamp which intersect the country. It is a toilsome drag over this Mount Misery ridge, and even the next swamp you encounter is a relief. At last, as MacBain's head station is approached, one begins to understand something of the really good soil of the South-East. First of all the ridges improve from scrub, sand, and stone, to a light sandy loam, thinly timbered with honeysuckle and sheaoak. Then there is another swampy belt, but with deeper and better soil and less limestone, and then a bank of excellent land upon which Mr. MacBean's homestead stands. Beyond this there is another swamp, intersected by narrow open banks of good soil, and a mile or two further on the indications of pent-up surface water begin to disappear even on the flats ; the grasses are finer, and flocks of

well-conditioned sheep scattered about the plains, and through the belts of open timber, present quite a new and welcome aspect. This is, in fact, the commencement of the good country of the Mosquito Plains. The soil for the first mile or two is a light black mould, and then it changes to a good red loam with a substrata of limestone, which here and there crops out on the surface. There are patches of timber, consisting chiefly of sheaoak, honeysuckle, and blackwood, but nearer Narracoorte there is more forest, and a strip of sandy country upon which the fern—one of the greatest banes of the South-East—has acquired undisputed possession.

In the foregoing descriptions of the country between Kingston and Narracoorte, I have of course referred particularly to the route I travelled, but almost the same words would answer for the whole extent of the Northern end of the district, excepting the Tatiara country. The swamps, or flats, and scrubby ridges which succeed one another so regularly almost from Kingston to MacBain's, run in nearly unbroken parallel lines from as far south as Mount Muirhead almost to Salt Creek on the north. Narracoorte, which is the practical centre of the Mosquito Plains country, is 51 miles distant from Kingston, and the red loam and limestone formation there is that which prevails upon the Plains, the exception being occasional wet flats, which occur irregularly, and strips of scrub and sand. There are some permanent streams of good water flowing through the Plains, the principal being the Narracoorte Creek, on which the township stands, and the Mosquito Creek, where Mr. John Robertson fixed his homestead many years ago, when the country was first settled, and upon which, and the Warattenbully country nearer the border, he has now acquired a magnificent estate. Narracoorte is computed to be 200 feet above the sea level, the rise from Kingston being gradual and continuous.

Reserving for the present what I have to say about the township of Narracoorte, its "land" question, and the famous caves which are the glory of the townsfolk, I will go on to the Tatiara. Leaving the township on a north-west line, you may canter pleasantly enough over the well-grassed and lightly-timbered country, which extends for some six miles to the boundary fences of Mr. Magarey's Narracoorte Station. Eastward of that track there is a belt of inferior sandy country ; but from the ridge where sand prevails to the wet flats on the westward there is a wide stretch of, for the most part, good red soil and limestone ; in fact the same formation I have already mentioned. This is undoubtedly good grazing country, and all of it, except where the limestone is too near the surface, or too plentiful to be cleared profitably, is also well adapted for the plough. Beyond Mr. Magarey's run is Morambra, certainly, as far as the quality of a large proportion of the land goes, one of the best stations in the South-East. The track winds round the base of a low range and crosses an open plain direct to the homestead. The plain itself, or the Morambra flat as it is called, presents a magnificent stretch of fine land, in which furrows miles long might be turned to-morrow. It extends from the foot of the range, westerly, for a distance varying, I should say, from one to two miles, and then you have again a strip of the long cutting grass, peculiar to most of the swampy ground. To the southward the plain stretches almost as far as the eye can reach, and the prospect it presents would cheer the heart of any bona fide cultivator seeking a section to settle upon,

if there were no landshark by to disturb his ruminations. It is possible that all this land may be occasionally covered with water in a very wet season, but even if so, it is evident it could be easily and inexpensively drained, as it lies on a higher level than the swamps on the westward. The soil is a light black loam, finely grassed, with only here and there a small patch of limestone to impede the progress of the plough, and at a very moderate computation I may safely say it presents, for settlement, from 5,000 to 7,000 acres of good agricultural land. Immediately at the base of the range I have mentioned, and on the eastern extremity of this plain, there is a belt of timber which presents a remarkable appearance, but one that I have since noticed in other parts of the South-East and even in the Western district of Victoria. The trees consist for the most part of gum and honeysuckle, with a few sheaoaks, and blackwoods. But the gums and even the gum saplings are all dead, although all the other trees rejoice in a strong and healthy growth. There is something weird-like in the ghastly barren whiteness of the withered trunks of the eucalypti, contrasting as they do with the fresh green of the honeysuckle, and the darker shades of the blackwood and sheaoak. I cannot pretend to account for the cause of this effect, for although several theories have been suggested to me, I scarcely think the true one has been discovered. It would be surely an interesting study for those who are learned in cognate matters to endeavor to ascertain why of all these trees which must once have lived as they now stand, side by side, the one race should have been so withered that they seem but an army of mere ghostly sentinels keeping watch over their comrades who survive.

To the northward of this open plain the country improves gradually and materially, until on the banks of the Cockatoo Lake, about a mile beyond the Morambra head station, the soil is richer of its class than any other I have seen in the South-East. On leaving the plain you have first of all a rather stiffer loam, with a few gums scattered here and there amongst the honeysuckles. Then as you approach the station the soil is richer and stronger and the timber larger and more abundant, until, for beauty of landscape and wealth of pasture, an area could be marked out worthy of comparison with the finest parks of England. There are swamps still on the eastward, and beyond the Cockatoo Lake the country gets worse again. Most of the land I saw on the next station, the Messrs. Laidlaw's, is decidedly inferior. On Padthaway, Mr. Lawson's station, the country varies from low-class scrub land to good stiff loamy soil, but on all I saw of the latter kind there was too much timber to render clearing for agricultural purposes a very tempting enterprise. From Padthaway to Swede's Flat is a dreary expanse of scrubby sandhills. Swede's Flat is a remarkable oval shaped depression in the centre of a chain of these scrubby rises, which would apparently receive all their drainage if their sandy surface permitted any to escape. The scrub extends altogether, from north of Padthaway to beyond Swede's Flat, for about 10 miles, and then approaching Mr. Binney's station the country gradually improves again. You cross first a strip of indifferent soil, undulating and lightly timbered, but around the homestead there is some good open forest land. The soil there is chiefly a stiffish red clay, well but not thickly timbered, and presenting occasionally the first indications of the Bay of Biscay surface which prevails on the clays of Tatiara.

The Tatiara country has long been celebrated as good, and it is indeed one of the "plums" of the South-East. Two Hundreds, in a block measuring 20 miles by 10, equal to 128,000 acres, might be laid out, which would include comparatively little inferior land. The soil is chiefly a strong red clay, and its waterlogged or Bay of Biscay surface is one evidence of its tenacity and retentiveness. It is well grassed, and presents alternate strips of open plain, and lightly timbered but scrubless country. There is plenty of heath and gum scrub on the outskirts of the district, but Tatiara proper is chiefly strong arable or grazing land—just such soil, in fact, as might be fairly expected to produce good crops of both wheat and roots, and possibly of clover. The country was originally taken up some quarter of a century ago, or thereabouts, by Mr. Binney, Mr. John Scott, and Mr. MacLeod. These gentlemen pushed manfully through the dreary desert from Wellington, having had intimations from the blacks of the land of promise which awaited them ; and a hill in the scrub, from which Mr. Binney obtained his first bird's eye survey of his destined settlement, is known to this day as " Binney's Look Out." Since then Mr. John Scott's " Carnawigara " run has changed owners, but Mr. Binney and Mr. MacLeod still hold their original stations. Hitherto the theodolite and chain of the surveyor have been but little known on Tatiara, but the day cannot be far distant when plenty of good agricultural sections will be obtainable there. Mr. MacLeod and Mr. Binney have each secured the freeholds of their head station sites, and those, with a few allotments at Border Town, represent, I believe, pretty nearly all the alienated land in the district. Carnawigara lies to the west of Border

Town, Wirrega (Mr. Binney's) to the south-west, and Nalang (Mr. MacLeod's) to the south.*

Border Town is destined, I believe, to acquire considerable commercial importance as the metropolis of a good agricultural district, but its greatness has all to come. When I visited it in June of last year it was neither elegant nor imposing in any of the features by which towns are usually judged, nor was it rich in the appearances which indicate the prosperity of centres of population. There was one essentially "bush" inn, which, I believe, has since closed its doors alike to weary wayfarers and unappreciative residents. There was also a store, a blacksmith's shop, some huts, a police-station, a dwelling-house, and one or two nondescript erections, the whole, including some other suburban huts, affording accommodation for a population of about 50 persons. But, notwithstanding the absence of present indications of much enterprise or progress, there is the one gratifying fact that the scanty population of Border Town, who now minister mainly to the requirements of some half-dozen sheep-stations, are located upon, and surrounded by good agricultural land,¹ which must soon be applied to its legitimate purpose. Of course, before this can be accomplished, and before the Government can expect to obtain a fair price for the land, facilities must be given, or guaranteed, for the conveyance of produce to the seaboard, but I can deal more appropriately with this part of the subject when I come to the consideration of the requirements of the district as a whole. At present the trade of the Tatiara, which consists almost exclusively of wool exports and stores imports, is divided between the various seaports of

the South-East and the Victorian over-landers. The bulk of the stores go either from Kingston or Robe, but the former place must inevitably become the port of export for Tatiara, because independently of its superior advantages as a harbor, it is considerably nearer to the country to be accommodated than any other port. Several hawkers from Victoria had made temporary squattages there. The place is seldom quite free from them, and some of the wool even from neighboring stations has been sent overland to Geelong for shipment. But these are matters only of the time. The era of progress has not even dawned yet upon Tatiara, but when the ball is once set rolling there, depend upon it it will have some rich sources from which to gather as it goes.

Passing to the southward of Nalang you soon encounter a range of scrubby sandhills, varied only by wet flats, coarsely grassed, and occasional banks of dry, light soil. The country is of this character to Conkar, an out-station of Mr. Henry Jones's. There it is chiefly open forest, but the soil is indifferent except in patches. At Binnum, Mr. Jones's head station, which is only some three miles from the border, the same description of country prevails. Although ordinary good grazing land, and not very heavily timbered, I am doubtful whether much of it could be profitably farmed. There is on the surface a shallow depth of a white hungry-looking marl, degenerating at places to absolute sand, but attaining in other veins all the stiffness of clay. There are also tracts of thick scrub in which mustering is exceedingly difficult. But the cream of the Binnum country is on Lake Cadnite, where there is somewhere about 40 square miles of strong red

* Mr. George Riddoch, of Penola, has recently purchased Nalang, and now holds the Station.

E

clay, similar to the Bay of Biscay lands of Tatiara, and which will afford another good agricultural district in the future. The lake is about six miles due east of the Conkar Station, and the good clay country lies also on the eastward of the ordinary track from Nalang.

I was surprised to learn from Mr. Jones that he and some of his neighbors suffered serious losses from the drought of 1865-6. Certainly, very few people thought of looking to the abundantly-watered South-East for evidence of losses from such a cause, and the Commissioners specially appointed to investigate the whole subject scarcely had it suggested to them that the drought had been felt injuriously south of Adelaide. But Mr. Jones complains that it was popularly supposed—by himself amongst others—that the enquiries of the Commissioners were limited to the Northern runs, and that the misconception was allowed to go unchallenged. At his special request I now proceed to give the particulars he supplied me with of the losses from the drought on Binnum and Conkar. Mr. Jones puts down those losses at 15,000 sheep and 800 cattle in actual deaths and loss of increase. He attributes the deaths partly to scarcity of feed, but chiefly to the scarcity of water, and he declares the runs to have been understocked at the time. He says that all the surface waters failed, and that waterholes were exhausted that had never been dry before. As another example, Mr. New, who held a small adjacent station, informed me that his losses during the same period from scarcity of feed and water were 1,500 sheep out of 5,000. I have given prominence to these statements because they were not included in the records of losses by the drought obtained by the Runs

Commission, and because they present quite a novel feature in South-Eastern experiences. Certainly, with the exception of the scrubby deserts on the extreme north of the district, the Binnum country is about the driest part of the South-East, but even there, if liability to droughts were considered at all probable, it would not be difficult to provide for the contingency, and I think it must have been rather from the absence of such provision, than from the inability to make it, that Mr. Jones's losses occurred.

There is another question of material importance to the pastoral settlers in the South-East, and of which Mr. Jones may be almost considered the apostle, which may, if only for that reason, be appropriately noticed now. I allude to the fencing improvements on runs. I suppose there is now scarcely an unfenced run in the district, and the consequently increased value of the stations is apparent in every respect. The settlers complain most bitterly that under the existing valuations they are not allowed for their fences, and that the Government will appropriate improvements of that description at the expiration of the leases. It has been, I believe, a rule with Mr. Goyder in estimating the value of fenced runs to base his assessment upon the natural grazing capabilities, and not upon the increased carrying power resulting from the fencing. But although this practice has protected the lessees from taxation upon their own improvements, I am at a loss to see that it justifies the non-allowance for fences at the expiration of a lease, as the principle of an allowance for improvements has been adopted by the Legislature. It seems inconsistent to allow a lessee several thousand pounds for a palatial residence, erected upon Crown lands, which to a new tenant may be unnecessary and comparatively valueless, and yet to withhold any consideration for the material, and, in fact, necessary improvement of boundary and subdivision fences. Of course the tenant will have reaped the benefit of his fences during the currency of his lease, but so he will equally of his mansion if he has built one, and of his woolshed and his wells, for which he is allowed. Suppose, for instance, a lessee, not being allowed anything for his fences, were, before the expiration of his lease, to take them all down or destroy them, I am not aware that he would be amenable to any penalty, and yet the value of the run to the next tenant, and consequently to the Government, would be seriously reduced. In fact, with the only exceptions of sinking for water, and the necessary buildings, fencing is the most necessary and valuable improvement upon station property, and other improvements being allowed for—some certainly less necessary—I cannot see why that should not be. I met with one case in the South-East, where a lessee, with only three years of his lease to run, had put up a subdivison post and wire fence seven miles in length, in the full knowledge that under the existing law he would be allowed nothing for it when his lease expired. He was satisfied, of course, that even in that three years it

would more than repay its cost, but that can hardly be held as justifying its appropriation by the Government without allowance, while the same gentleman is now actually receiving an allowance of several thousand pounds, in the form of a reduced rental, for a fine two-storey stone house, which may be largely in excess of the domestic requirements of the next tenant. Of course the fencing on some runs might also be inconsistent with the purposes of a new tenant; but the Government Valuators might be fairly entrusted with the responsibility of determining, at the expiration of the leases, what were reasonable and necessary lines of fencing, and what would be their then value to the incoming tenant. And this value the outgoing tenant may surely fairly claim from his successor.

South of Binnum, towards the stations of Mr. Affleck and Mr. Adam Smith, the country gets gradually better. On Mr. Affleck's there is some fine open country, with a more loamy and friable soil than on Binnum, although much of it is of the same class as there ; and at Mr. Smith's you have again the red loam and limestone of the Mosquito Plains. Thence into Narracoorte the same formation prevails, varied only, as on the west of the township, with a strip of sandy, scrubby country.

CHAPTER VII.

NARRACOORTE AND KINCRAIG—RIVAL TOWNSHIPS—LOCAL INSTITUTIONS—TRADE AND TRAFFIC—THE STALACTITE CAVES OF NARRACOORTE—OUR LAND SYSTEM, AND SUGGESTIONS FOR ITS REFORM.

THE spirit of rivalry which predominates in the British mind is largely developed in the movement which, being in fact the opposition of a new Government township to an older one established by private enterprise, may be briefly designated—Narracoorte versus Kincraig. Many years ago, in the days of the early settlement of the Mosquito Plains, an enterprising settler laid out on purchased land the present township of Kincraig. Although the site was not a happily chosen one, the allotments were readily purchased, and houses, shops, stores, and other buildings incidental to a thriving rural township were erected from time to time. A considerable population was attracted to the spot, vested interests were developed there, and people naturally arranged their plans, and built their houses with some degree of faith in the permanence of the existing town. But presently the Government proclaimed a new township on the west of Kincraig. It was dubbed Narracoorte, and at a distance of rather more than half a mile from the nearest, and about a mile from some of the houses and places of business in Kincraig, a handsome, spacious, and convenient series of buildings, comprising a Police-Station, a Post-Office, a Telegraph Office, and a Local Court House were erected. There is consequently a gap of about three-quarters of a mile between these necessary offices and the centre of business; for although most of the Government allotments were taken up by an Adelaide speculator, local men still build their shops and stores and houses where local business is concentrated. The Government have removed the business of the Telegraph Office to the new and distant buildings; the police are located there, and the Local Court has been proclaimed. But although the new Post-Office is complete, and its conveniences of space and arrangement sadly required in Kincraig, the authorities have not yet screwed up the courage to compel the residents in the actual township to walk three quarters of a mile to the supposed one, to post a letter or buy a twopenny stamp. This being so, it will be readily understood that, however well the official arrangements may be adapted to the future progress of Narracoorte they do not at all satisfy the present population of Kincraig. Indeed, but for this unfortunate division Kincraig would be already a very convenient, and even handsome town. Many well-looking structures are already erected, and their tasteful fronts and satisfactory proportions speak volumes—as indeed do many buildings in other parts of the South-East—of the skill of Mr. Gore, who may be considered as the District Architect. Two large new stores are in course of erection, one for Mr. H. Jones, and the other for Messrs. Fuller & Webb; but neither is within the Government boundary road. Of course the rivalry which the competitors—represented by pretty nearly all the local residents on the one side, and by the Government and their speculating buyers on the other—sustain, crops out in other directions, and some time ago opinions waxed opposite and warm as to the direction in which a new piece of road intended to connect Kincraig with the main thoroughfares to Penola and Kingston was taken. The case, as put to me, was that the road, as adopted by the Local Road Board and actually made, involved the construction of 103 chains, comprising a heavy piece of cutting and a bridge, whereas 75 chains would have sufficed to connect the main road to the border with the main road to Kingston in a straight line, avoiding also both the heavy cutting and the bridge, the Penola-road running into this line at a right angle. Certainly the road as made does twist about in a most eccentric manner, and forms a very unnecessary elbow. But at all events it serves the useful purpose of affording a metalled roadway not only through some of the bye-ways of Kincraig, but from thence to the remote buildings which the Government have erected in the midst of a beggarly array of unoccupied allotments. The pains of the pilgrimage thereto, which, till lately, had to be performed over heavy sand, is consequently somewhat diminished, and the Kincraigites chuckle as they tell you that that same piece of road has already cost the Government far more than the Narracoorte allotments realised.

In other respects Kincraig is not much behind other purely pastoral towns, and when it becomes, as it inevitably must, the centre of a good agricultural district, its progress will be proportionately great. It has already a good Institute, and efforts are being made to obtain a resident clergyman of the Established Church. From the hill which rises abruptly on the south, a good view of the surrounding country may be obtained. It is through this hill that the cutting I have mentioned has been made, and it affords a good opportunity of examining the various strata which prevail there. On the highest part of the rise there is only a very shallow depth of good, but light loamy soil on the surface. Below that there is a bed of conglomerate of sandstone and limestone, then a layer of soft sandstone, and below that again a flinty congealed limestone, which proves a very hard and useful road metal. On the flats around the township, and generally, except on the very tops of the rises, there is a greater depth of top soil, and where the limestone crops up too abundantly to permit profitable clearing for the plough is quite exceptional on the lower levels. Immediately on the north and west of the township there is a narrow belt of hilly but sandy country, which I have already mentioned, and to which the foregoing remarks do not of course apply. It is not particularly creditable to the past legislation of our provincial statesmen that Victoria should still command the larger proportion of the trade of Kincraig. Melbourne go-a-headism, not to call it enterprise, still retains a commercial field which should be exclusively South Australian. Representatives of Victorian houses dash through the district at their pleasure, with well-bred "pair" teams and livery servants in attendance, in splendidly-appointed waggonettes, designed to carry superabundant "samples" of expensive goods, which, openly evading South Australian duties, find their way into the stocks of local storekeepers at prices which would be absolutely unprofitable to Adelaide merchants, whose bagsmen plod humbly and wearisomely from township to township in the wretched mail conveyances which Cobb and Co. still retain upon the South-Eastern roads. Of course these are circumstances which are rather indicative than creative; but the real obstacle to the extension of South Australian trade here lies, of course, in the non-development of the means of communication which ought to exist between inland centres of industry and population and the nearest and best seaport. Gradually, no doubt, the thing will find its own level, but a timely impetus from what should be the fostering care of a paternal Government would facilitate that progress in a most welcome and material degree. For instance, a licensed victualler recently settled at Kincraig told me he had received goods from MacDonnell Bay, for which he paid for cartage £5 per ton; from Guichen Bay, £5 10s. per ton; and from Lacepede Bay, £3 10s. per ton. But then under existing circumstances, there is the material disadvantage against the latter place, that it has no regular steam communication with Melbourne or Adelaide, which both the other ports possess. And you are told too, not only that Melbourne houses can undersell our Adelaide traders—a fact, if it be one, upon which His Honor Mr. Commissioner Noel could probably throw some light—but that in the Melbourne markets there are larger assortments, newer fashions, and greater elegance and variety to choose from. But, be all this as it may, I can trace another cause which has had a baneful influence for South Australia in the past, and which certainly is attributable to the sleepy-headedness of our legislators. Until last year four days and a half were occupied in the conveyance of mails and passengers from the South-East to Adelaide, whereas the over-land journey to Melbourne, in far more comfortable conveyances, was accomplished in two days, and only one night actually spent on the road. This necessarily operated as a virtual barrier between Adelaide and the South-East; and even the settlers around Narracoorte preferred a trip to Melbourne rather than to their own metropolis proper when the slack season gave them an opportunity of a "spell" in town. Use is second nature, and the habit of going to Melbourne in preference to Adelaide naturally enough resulted in the establishment of business relations there also, until the transactions of these South Australian settlers with South Australia were, and are still, pretty nearly confined to the payment of rents and assessments, or purchase-money for land. Thus it was that the same supineness which is still, by its negative effect, forcing the Murray trade of South Australia up stream to Echuca, crippled the commercial enterprise of Adelaide on what ought to have been, and may even yet be, a profitable field for its development. A reform has indeed been accomplished in the time occupied by mail conveyances between Adelaide and the South-East, but customs which have sprung from the practice of years are not often broken down with ordinary efforts. Adelaide legislation must now do more than merely accelerate the conveyance of mails and passengers before South Australia will regain the commercial vantage ground she has lost in the South-East. And it is after all gratifying to know that our governing powers are beginning to recognise the importance of this fact.

There is one feature of the Narracoorte district which I altogether despair of doing justice to. I allude to its famous and wonderful stalactite caverns. They, of course, constitute the "show" *par excellence* of the country side, but it perhaps detracts from the chance of an adequate appreciation of their wonders, and their supernatural beauties, that visitors are usually, as I was, inducted to the view of them under the hospitable but somewhat contradictory influences of bottled porter, pigeon pies, or some other unpoetical solids, sparkling Moselle and picnic accompaniments generally. The landlord of the "Commercial" at Kincraig, with a shrewd idea of business, pleasantly combined with patriotic pride, has had a waggonette built expressly for "picnics to the Caves." And there are always plenty of enthusiastic residents ready to play the host and chaperone wondering strangers to these mystic solitudes in the very bowels of the earth, where nature has given an uncontrolled rein to the silent and unseen workers in her laboratory of beauty. The party it was my good ' fortune to be invited to join were tooled to the scene of our explorations by an artistic whip, in a four-in-hand drag kindly placed at our disposal by a gentleman of the neighborhood. The caves are situated some five or six miles to the south or south-east of Narracoorte, and, after leaving the Penola-road, the route lies through the scrub, over a scarcely defined and uncleared track. As you approach the spot, you enter a jumble of low hills, about the appearance of which, as seen from the surface of the earth, there is nothing whatever remarkable. Outcroppings of limestone here and there, the ordinary stunted timber peculiar to gum and honeysuckle scrubs, with a thick undergrowth of ferns, and a light red surface soil, varied by occasional patches of sand, make up an outside scenic aspect which may be met with in fifty other localities in the South-East, and is certainly by no means suggestive of the sights

in store. Even when your driver rounds up his team on the open summit of a low irregular-shaped hillock, your first curious glance reveals but little beyond broken bottles, and empty tins that once held lobsters or sardines, to indicate the vicinity of the caves. But look again, and you will see— well, to use a plain term, a hole ; and really, so far, that is all. Here we are, then, on the threshold of one of the wonders of Australia, if not of the world. A cold-blooded philosopher would probably stretch his legs, and quietly discuss a weed and a glass of Bass's bitter, as a judicious preparation for the exertions awaiting him. But a hot-headed enthusiast would of course blunder into the hole, and make a rush for the marvels to be revealed. You may easily descend this first hole, and it leads you to a large underground chamber, which being fully lighted at both ends, thickly strewn with every imaginable relic of picnic and convivial parties generally, and overgrown with a wild and rank vegetation at its entrances, presents nothing very remarkable even to the enthusiast. Imagine an unfinished boring for a huge and lofty cellar, in a very slovenly condition of disorder and incompleteness, weeds here, and litter of all kinds there, but after all with a roof of rare but half obliterated beauty which you scarcely notice in the mess which prevails, and you will have some idea of the first of the caves, and perhaps agree with me in thinking that after all a pint of Bass won't be a bad thing before we go any further. I believe at any rate an interlude of the kind is generally observed here, and it is only charitable to forewarn future visitors that it is a really prudent precaution to fortify their powers of endurance for the exertion their explorations will entail. Now, then, to resume our way. Beyond the second aperture in the roof which terminates the first cave, and admits a flood of daylight to the entrance to the next, you may discern, where the light mingles softly with subterranean darkness, massive columns, weird-like forms, eccentric images, grotesque designs, and figures of you know not what grouped here and scattered there. Everything is uncertain and indefinite; inconsistent and purposeless in detail; and yet blending marvellously as a whole, as much beyond the descriptive powers of any ordinary quill driver as the glories of a tropical sunset, or the fanciful wreathings of smoke-puffs from your pipe, exceed the best limner's art. In either case, upon the basis of the irregular wealth of beauty that is presented, fancy may portray wondrous but immaterial pictures, perfect to the eye, and bewildering to the mind, but their reproduction, in any adequate degree, in print or in color, would be a hopeless task. A very little distance within this second chamber, lighting candles or torches is the order of the day, and then a new aspect is given to the scene. Other figures, indiscernible before come gradually into relief, and rich and varying tints are disclosed on the stalactites that stud the roof, or droop in fretted beauty to the floor. And you detect the openings of other corridors of these subterranean palaces, guarded by stalagmites you may mistake for sculptured images of Gog and Magog, borrowed from Guildhall, or narrow but treacherous chasms that if you cross will make you appreciate a clear eye, a firm hand, and a steady foot. Enter the first of these, and recognise other entrances to other chambers, and you will find your ideas as to the number and order of the caves getting pretty well adrift. So it was with me at any rate, and I cannot pretend to any exactness as to how many cavernous chambers I entered, or in which one of the series it was that I saw the Strangwayian gridiron, intended to be an iron-barred gate, which failed to protect the petrified remains of the blackfellow, who years agone crept into those dark recesses, away from his Christian hunters, and finally laid down to die in the nook where the Showman found him. No wonder that petrifaction preserved his body from decay, nor that the prize it presented was wrested from the frivolous protection designed by Mr. Strangways when revelling in the full tide of the now receded glories of his Commissionership. I don't know how long life could be sustained there, but it is a great relief to escape from the numbing influences which almost insensibly affect you to the fresh free air and the bright light of day. It would occupy more than a day to examine thoroughly all the caves that have been already discovered and explored. No sooner do you regain the surface and re-oxygenise your lungs than your enthusiastic guides will point to another descent, more difficult than the first, inducting you to another series of caves where, to make good your way to all that is to be seen, you must sometimes clamber up steep and slippery walls of stalagmite, or crawl upon all-fours through a tunnel better adapted to the passage of an eel than a man. Marvellous tales of course are told of incidents that have happened there, but most marvellous of all is the story of how several prominent members of the late Ministry of all the Rotundities (Messrs. A. Blyth, W. Milne, and T. English) got through that tunnel and back again. Another speciality is the "bat" cave, where countless numbers of actual bats have made a secluded home, and where you sink knee deep in guano that has accumulated through unknown time. You may pursue your climbings and crawlings almost indefinitely if you are curious and venturesome enough, and finally return to the world once more by an aperture several hundred yards from that by which you entered.

There is one circumstance in connection with these caves that is very much to be deplored. All the choicest stalactites have been chipped to virtual destruction for the sake of specimens to be taken away, and there is scarcely a perfect petrifaction to be found. But as the process of exudation and congealing is constantly going on, the present defects would be largely remedied in time if further spoliation were prohibited. By-and-bye, as population increases around Narracoorte, and the attractions of the caves become more widely known, it may be worth while to declare a reserve and appoint a keeper who might supplement his income by levying a small charge for acting as a guide to visitors.

One other question remains to be dealt with before I close my notes of Narracoorte, because there are reasons why what it is necessary to say about it may be more appropriately introduced in connection with the Mosquito Plains than any other part of the district. The question is "Our Land System," and the relevancy it has to the Mosquito Plains consists in the fact that they will afford a large contribution to future land sales in the South-East. At the Mount Gambier end of the district the area of volcanic soil is almost entirely alienated from the Crown, and at Kalangadoo, and around Penola, the pick of the land has been secured by private holders. But there are large areas of good agricultural land on the Plains, and in other localities I have already described, which—to say nothing of the rich swamp soils now in

course of reclamation by the drainage—will be very soon available for purchase. An idea may be formed of the rapidity with which surveys are being pushed on from the fact that twelve parties are now* at work in the South-East. Eight of these are surveying lands for sale, two are levelling for the drainage works at Mount Muirhead and on the Woakwine, and two are laying out the new line of road from Salt Creek to Narracoorte. The land surveys are going on to the north, south-east, east, and east-south-east of Narracoorte, to the north-east of Mr. Robertson's Mosquito Creek Station, on Wrattanbully and Kilbride, and in the Hundred of Hindmarsh. There will, therefore, be a large extent of surveyed land ready for sale very soon, and the bulk of it will be available for farming purposes. The importance of this fact is increased by the climatic advantages of the South-East, which render the district, where the land is good, the best outlet for the cramped agricultural enterprise of the colony. The value of the district to South Australia in this sense is not sufficiently understood. For my own part I utterly reject the new fear, uttered the other day, that we have too many farmers in the colony, or that farming in South Australia won't pay. If the colony is to progress—if the wealth of the soil is to be developed—we must foster and extend agricultural industry. In fact, if we are to make the most of what we have got, we must farm where we can. And to ensure this being done it is the duty and obligation of the State, or of those who hold the helm, to give every legitimate facility that will promote the settlement of agricultural lands for agricultural purposes. The South-Eastern District supplies one essential condition, in large areas of unsold land where both soil and climate are better adapted to agricultural purposes

F   * March, 1868.

than in any other portion of the colony. The other condition, viz., facilities for the settlement of these lands for agricultural purposes, rests entirely with our land system, and the question which must be considered—and practically handled, too, before these lands are thrown into the market, as they soon will be, is simply—Does our existing land system afford those facilities to the desired and fullest possible extent, or does it not? The answer, if given conscientiously, whether by land agent, land jobber, squatter, speculator, or farmer, must be in the negative. The proof is that the system as it stands has practically driven the bona fide farmer from the land market proper to the land agent if he has money enough to buy, and to the land-jobber if he wants a little of that particular help which deferred payments would afford him. Such a circumstance as an individual wanting to get one, two, or three hundred acres to settle upon for farming purposes, and with just money enough to buy them and carry on his business, walking into the auction-room and getting such land as he wants at a fair price—the issue of genuine competition with men like himself—without the intervention of the sharks that were generated by the system, and have fattened upon it ever since, is unheard of now-a-days. And yet that is exactly what our land system ought to ensure. I am justified, then, in saying that it has failed and requires amendment. But, after all, very few people deny that. A good many, it is true, when reform is suggested to them, without venturing to dispute the necessity, shrug their shoulders in complacent disregard of the possibility of effecting it. Capital, they imply, if they do not say, will always conquer. Well, capital is a very good and pleasant thing —good for individuals to possess and for countries to attract, but confound it when it impedes instead of helps, retards instead of encourages the advancement of a community. When the power of capital is used to sustain monopoly and selfishness, the State, as after all the superior power, is justified in breaking down the conditions which permit the monopoly, and encourage selfishness. Far better to drive a few thousands of foreign capital to seek new channels for investment than to allow it to thwart the purposes of the State, and the best principles of colonization, by dictating, as it practically does now, its own terms to farmers who want land to settle on.

If it is admitted, then, that the first principle of our land system should be to promote that particular description of settlement that will ensure the extraction of the full value of the soil, and the sustenance of the largest and most productive population, from which the greatest measure of material wealth and permanent prosperity will flow, the necessity for land reform is established. The difficulty is to secure an amendment that, without exposing the country to worse evils, will cure those that have been demonstrated in the past. Some of the *nostrums* which have been advocated would, I think, do infinitely more harm than good, for certainly they would create mischief tenfold more rapidly than they would eradicate it. For instance, as proposed,* to throw open areas of land

---

* By Mr. Alexander Hay, M.P., an extensive land buyer, who has propounded a scheme for throwing open certain areas to free selection with deferred payments, at £1 per acre with conditions of residence and occupation ; but *who also proposes to retain*, in unchecked operation on other areas, and without conditions, the *present Auction system !* Such an alteration would manifestly increase the existing advantages of the capitalist and speculator.

at the arbitrary price of £1 per acre, would inevitably involve us, as a people, in the land mess which has become as painful as it is patent in Victoria; and after all, by merely cheapening the land you but increase the adverse power of capital, which Mr. Hay no doubt understands as well as most people. And worst of all, if you proclaimed an area which must be sold for £1 per acre, and no more nor less, it would certainly include some sections better worth £2 or £3 per acre, than others would be worth the £1, or even less. Of course there would be what are called *simultaneous* applications for the prize allotments; and then *drawing lots* under the auspices of the Government, or in plain terms, State gambling, must be resorted to; the lucky drawer, who would as probably be a fair counterpart of the Victorian "medium" as a bona fide settler, could dispose of his lot to a monopolising squatter of the locality, or any speculating capitalist who might secure him. It would be impossible to administer a system which embraced an arbitrary price for land, whether worth more or less, without some such unsatisfactory and injurious result as this. I am not, however, going to carp at the system as it is, or at the remedies which are proposed, without contributing something to the stock of suggestions that have been made. I believe thoroughly in the sufficiency of the reform I propose, and I hope I don't do so altogether on the principle which makes us think so frequently that all our geese are swans.

First of all I propose, as the fundamental basis of any righteous reform that can be adopted, a CLASSIFICATION OF ALL UNSOLD LANDS. Three classes would be sufficient—First, agricultural; second, pastoral; third, scrub. A Board, to consist of the Surveyor-General and two other competent officers, might be safely entrusted with the responsibility of classification. Then, as subsidiary principles, let none but agricultural lands be sold outright, for the present at all events. Let pastoral lands be leased, and scrub be dealt with under the provisions of the present Scrub Lands Act, an extension of its schedule being all that would be necessary in that respect.

As to the sale of agricultural lands, it being conceded—or if not I am prepared to maintain—that the object of the State, acting in the interest of the community, should be to secure their agricultural settlement, I would advocate certain conditions of sale being imposed which would effect the purpose. I know that astute people say you cannot sell land in fee and exact conditions. Then withhold the grant; give in fact only an agreement to sell—which would have just as good a value—until the conditions were fulfilled. Let those conditions be, in fact, agricultural occupation, implying a proportion of tillage during a given term, on pain of forfeiture. The upset price of all these lands should be determined by valuation by the classifiers; competition, in cases of two or more simultaneous applications, should be by tender instead of auction; and deferred payments granted, under due supervision, when applied for, at a fixed rate of interest, for a term to be limited. I hold that all these innovations may be justified in detail, and that in their operation as a whole, they would confine the competition for agricultural lands to those who would be bona fide agricultural occupiers. To examine them in detail, few, I think, can deny that classification is desirable, or that it is manifestly absurd to deal with good agricultural lands on precisely the same conditions that are applied to land which, however good for pastoral purposes, never can be farmed. Mr. Charles Goode, I believe, originated the idea, when he represented East Torrens ; but, at all events, it is too good and too well adapted to our present requirements to be relinquished. Then as to conditions of sale or agreement to sell. If lands are sold avowedly for the promotion of agricultural settlement, people who buy with an honest bona fide intent will not be hampered by conditions necessary to their business, and those who don't want to be farmers are not wanted to bid. The determination of the upset price by fair valuation will protect the public interests from possible combination, and cannot injure the honest buyer. Competition by tender, with or without valuation, would, I am inclined to think, be an improvement on sale by auction, as materially increasing the difficulties of mere speculating bidders. For instance, a case has come to my knowledge, within the last few days, of a professed land reformer and poor man's friend, who attended a recent land sale with a big bank account to back him, and after running up other bidders until certain sections were knocked down to him, directly afterwards offered them to one of the bidders he had opposed, at a considerable advance, double an ordinary agent's purchasing fee, on the lot. This is one of the very worst forms of land jobbery, and the auction system can never altogether evade it. But competition by tender would be a great stumbling block in the way of the gentry who practise these dodges one day, and prate of Land Reform the next. It may of course be objected that even a Tender Board might be tampered with, but 1 don't despair of finding honest men, who, in such a capacity, would vindicate with equal zeal their own honor and the

interests of the public. Then finally as to deferred payments, I can see no objection to them, if they are not made compulsory. The capitalist farmer may say, I have the money to pay your price, and I don't want to pay you interest. Then let him pay his cash, but still under the penalty for non-compliance with conditions. But the man who wants to buy, and time to pay in, may be fairly and reasonably accommodated by the State, who would have ample security, and who would exact a sufficient, but still by comparison with a money lender's rate, a moderate interest.

Then, secondly, as to leasing pastoral lands. The conditions of tenure for many years to come have been fixed by recent legislation in certain districts beyond the line of rainfall drawn by Mr. Goyder. In other districts, on the expiry of the leases, the auction test comes in. But there is one saving clause—the power of resumption. Now, while I maintain that pastoral lands which are not in any sense agricultural should not be forced into the market merely for the purposes of revenue, but that as they will improve by grazing they should be leased for grazing purposes, I also deny the right of the squatter to complain if his run is resumed for the benefit of the farmer. I urge, then, the desirability of resuming leases of pastoral lands adjacent to agricultural areas, and cutting them up into smaller blocks, to be leased in proportionate areas as grazing farms to bona fide purchasers and occupiers of agricultural sections. The South-East offers peculiar facilities for the initiation of a system of this kind, because there strips of land that will never be available for agriculture, constantly intersect the better land, that is.

The Scrub Lands I would deal with as I have said under the provisions of the existing Act, the main principles of which are liberal and judicious. I have now pointed out what I consider to be the defects of the existing system, and I have carefully enumerated the remedies I propose. I believe, while avoiding the evils of the Victorian system, they would be, in practice, encouraging and beneficial to the bona fide farmer, and a sufficient and wholesome check to the monopolist and the speculator.

CHAPTER VIII.

SWAMPS AND WET FLATS—RECLAMATION BY DRAINAGE—MR. GOYDER'S SCHEME—THE COURSE OF THE DRAINS—THEIR EFFICIENCY—THE NATURE OF THE SOIL RECLAIMED—FACILITIES FOR SETTLEMENT AND EXPORT.

In the preceding chapters of this work allusion has been made to the vast areas of swamp and wet flats which extend almost from the southernmost corner of the district to its northern extremity at Salt Creek, and even there unite with the Coorong. I have described already the general features of the wet lands extending northward from Guichen Bay, and eastward to the Mosquito Plains; and the outlines of the scheme for completing the drainage of those areas have also been indicated. But now I am able to write with much greater detail of description and certainty of conclusion of the great work of reclamation which has been wisely undertaken, and is being vigorously prosecuted to the southward of Guichen Bay and the Plains. When I first saw the works in progress in June of 1867 the scheme was not fully developed, except in theory, in even an experimental stage. Now after the lapse of little more than a year enough has been accomplished in actual result to demonstrate its practical success. Hitherto the public even of our own colony have altogether failed to realise the extent and importance of the undertaking, and of the influence it must have upon the future progress of the district; but that has been rather from the absence of information than from any unwillingness to set a proper value upon such an enterprise. In fact, even in the South-Eastern District itself there is a very limited knowledge, and an inadequate conception of what has been already done. It has often been remarked that the people of Adelaide know very little of Mount Gambier, and that the slight appreciation they have has only been evinced very recently; but if the metropolis of the colony has afforded few visitors, except bagsmen or tax-gatherers in various guises, to the acknowledged "garden" of South Australia, certainly the rich lands which are now being rapidly wrested from the wasteful grasp of superabundant water, have been to a great extent a *terra incognita* to the majority of even south-eastern settlers. Traditions have been woven, and legends constructed, of

" Moving accidents by flood and field ;
Of hair-breadth 'scapes"

upon some treacherous swamp, or boggy flat ; predictions are uttered even now of the recurrence of certain wet seasons of a quarter of a century ago, when bets were offered to navigate a boat across country from the Dismal Swamp to Goolwa ; but the real capabilities of the lands which have been water-ridden so long, are scarcely understood as they might have been even in the district which includes them. I have, however, profitted by a favorable opportunity to make myself acquainted by personal examination with the lands the drainage will reclaim, and I have seen practical and absolute proof of the capacity of the drains to answer the purpose for which they are intended. If, therefore, in the descriptions I have to give of the land, and of the drains, I write with the positiveness of conviction, and reject as being scarcely worth the words it takes to tell them some of the ingenious doubts and fears which sceptics, cavillers, and croakers express about the success of the scheme, it is because I have actually seen the conclusions of able and impartial men, to whom the credit of the conception and execution of the work so far as it has gone belongs, abundantly verified by evidence so practical as to be unassailable, and yet so simple as to be plain to the understanding of a child.

I scarcely think it necessary to write anything in justification of such a work being submitted to a practical test. If possible to effect, it must be desirable. The reclamation of essentially waste lands and the conversion of them to some useful and profitable purpose, even in so large a territory as this, would under almost any circumstances be commendable and beneficial, but in this instance there is a combination of special advantages which does not often occur when similar schemes are projected in even older settled countries. The land is remarkably rich, the climate

is better adapted to agriculture than in any other part of the colony, and facilities for the conveyance and export of produce are at hand, and may be easily turned to account. I make these statements with a thorough conviction of their absolute correctness, and I shall take care to substantiate them all in detail as I go on.

First of all, in order that those who are unacquainted with the physical configuration of the district may clearly understand the basis upon which Mr. Goyder has proceeded in the construction of his scheme, it is necessary to describe the superficial features he has had to deal with more particularly than I have done in preceding articles. I will begin with the coast line, which from Cape Northumberland to Cape Jaffa follows mainly a north-west course, and excepting only the indentation which forms the northern extremity of Lacepede Bay, it trends still to the west of north to the mouth of the Murray. A low ridge of sandhills flanks the coast-line, with scarcely a break from the point where Lake Bonney has its outlet in the sea, about 18 miles N.W. of Cape Northumberland to Cape Lannes at Guichen Bay. Northward of that point this coast ridge dies away in very insignificant rises. But returning again to our southern starting point, and going only some five miles inland, we encounter a ridge of something better than sand although confessing kindred thereto, which also extends in one unbroken line from a point east of Lake Bonney very nearly to Lake Eliza within about a dozen miles of Guichen Bay. Further inland other ranges follow exactly the same course, running from S.E. to N.W., parallel with the coast-line, with open flats between them, their elevation increasing in the most regular order to the eastward, and forming in fact a series of terraces which present a vast natural staircase from the sea. But it is the ridge running from east of Lake Bonney to Lake Eliza—the first of the series eastward of the coast ridge of sand hummocks—that we have mainly to consider now. Remember, if you please, that it runs from S.E. to N.W., and is unbroken, naturally, throughout its entire length of some 45 or 50 miles. The other ranges to the eastward on the contrary are not unbroken, for although they preserve in the main the parallel course I have indicated, there are gaps through which the waters of a higher or more easterly flat (the terms are synonymous) find an easy and natural outlet. Of course, as each succeeding range and flat rises to the eastward the natural fall is to the west, and all these points being borne in mind, the normal condition of things prior to the initiation of the drainage scheme may be easily understood. The whole of the surplus waters—by which I mean all that the soil itself could not absorb or the ordinary channels of surface drainage receive — of the higher levels to the eastward followed its natural fall westward to the coast until intercepted by the unbroken ridge extending from Lake Bonney to Lake Eliza. It may be as well to explain here that this ridge is known at its southern end as Glen's Range—from the fact that the Mayurra Station held by Mr. George Glen is situated upon it—and to the north of Rivoli Bay as the Woakwine Range. At this point the waters congregating from the eastward and unable to find an outlet to the sea, were turned to the north-west, and with a very slight fall they moved slowly down the flat belts lying between the ridges I have named as running parallel with the coast, replenishing many of the coast lakes—terminating with Lake Hawdon—by the way, and

finally passing over the Biscuit Flat past Mount Benson to the Maria Creek Swamp, and escaping to the sea by Maria Creek, or to the Coorong by the upper channels of the Reedy Creek. Thus it happened that a vast extent of flat country lying between the regularly recurring ranges north of Lake Bonney was flooded every year, not only by its own heavy rainfall but by the waters from higher levels checked in their natural fall by Glen's or the Woakwine Range.

Plainly there was a great evil in this. The country, whatever its value might otherwise have been, presented only a dreary waste of water for some months of the year, and was but of questionable worth when the floods subsided for a time. Some authorities, rightly or wrongly I cannot determine, but certainly with some show of feasibility, attribute the prevalence of coast disease to the noxious exhalations arising from the swamp waters. But be this as it may, even as you may have too much of most good things, there was certainly too much of water here. Presently it was found that the efficient working of the line of telegraph to Victoria was seriously impeded by the superabundant water. The line had been constructed in its direct course to Mount Gambier across the Biscuit, and along the Mount Muirhead flats, and it was a common thing for the line Inspectors to make long journeys through water up to, and sometimes over their saddle flaps. At last one officer, ordered to inspect the line in a more than ordinarily wet season, pleaded that the task would entail his being drowned, which he objected to. He was left to choose between compliance and resignation. He resigned, and another officer, who undertook the duty, was compelled to give it up as a bad job. Then it began to be apparent that the telegraph line could not be worked where it was, and that it would have to be reconstructed on the ridge running parallel with the flat. And then, too, it began to be seriously considered officially whether, as another alternative, the water could not be got rid of, and the telegraph line retained where it was, and is, and will continue to be. It is not an easy matter to determine now with whom the idea absolutely originated, but the credit of its subsequent expansion and present realisation, in both design and execution, belongs undoubtedly to Mr. George Woodroffe Goyder, the Surveyor-General of South Australia. But it is only fair to mention that Mr. W. A. Crouch, of Mount Gambier, who was one of the earliest settlers at Rivoli Bay, when a township was actually established there, had already identified his name with the drainage of the district by repeatedly urging upon the Government the desirability of undertaking the work. The Hon. William Milne, too, may claim the distinction of having been the first Commissioner of Crown Lands to give a warm and earnest measure of Ministerial sanction and assistance to the project. In the early part of 1863 he made an official visit to the district, accompanied by Mr. Goyder and Mr. William Hanson, then the Engineer-in-Chief, and from that time he has zealously supported the design whenever the power to do so efficiently has been in his hands. But for the design as it is now being executed, and for its practical success, Mr. Goyder deserves all the praise. The planning, direction, and responsibility of the whole work have been entailed upon him in addition to his ordinary official duties, and it will be seen from the particulars I have to record of what has been already actually accomplished, how skilfully and energetically he has carried out the work, and how thoroughly he deserves the gra-

titude of the public for the grand results he has ensured.

From the moment that it was resolved to attempt the drainage of this vast area of swamp and flat it was a comparatively simple matter to determine at what point the experiment should be commenced. The pent up waters were in fact as index hands upon the dial plate of nature. Their fall to the Woakwine Range, and its effect as an unbroken natural dam arresting their progress to the sea, and turning their slow course to the northwest, were so plainly indicated that to cut through that range and give an immediate outlet following the fall was obviously the first necessary step. Fortunately, too, it was easy to determine where that cut should be made; for at a point where the Cootel Swamp indented itself into the range, and formed a huge natural reservoir, filled every year to a depth of some ten feet on its western side, the range itself, as the consequence of this indentation, was narrowed to a mere strip, involving but a few chains of cutting to give the swamp waters on its eastern side an outlet to Lake Frome on the west. Here then it was determined a commencement should be made, and the late Mr. Coulthard, then the Resident-Engineer for the district, was entrusted with the work. A cutting was made in October, 1863, through this "narrow neck" as it is called, four feet deep, 12 feet wide, and eight chains, or 528 feet long. At that time all else that was done was the formation of a few surface races —they could hardly be called drains—intersecting the swamp tapped by the cutting. Certainly this was not much, but it was a commencement, and it sufficed to indicate the success that would reward the execution of a well-planned scheme for completing the drainage of the district. The immediate effect was to let off an immense body of water that had heretofore filled the Ocotel Swamp, or moved slowly to the north-west along the course of the Biscuit Flat. As far north as Maria Creek—where another small channel to which I have referred in an earlier chapter* was partially cut at about the same time—the effect was perceptible in the diminution of the water on the swamp there, and in fact on all the wet country lying between the two points. And wherever this effect could be traced it was clearly beneficial. Some of the slight rises on the flats that used to be covered as the waters moved down from the south, were "reclaimed," and finer grasses appeared as the result of the absence of water and the possibility of grazing there. And even where this was not the case the wet country was decidedly, if in a less degree, improved for grazing purposes, as I have already pointed out in my descriptions of Lake Hawdon and other places, by the fact of the water being reduced and consequently disappearing so much earlier in the year.

For some time after this very little was done towards the extension of the works until the whole matter was placed in Mr. Goyder's hands,† and from that moment the commencement of the drainage scheme as a complete, consistent, and proved work must be dated. What had been done before was well enough as far as it went, and about the propriety of

making a cutting at the Narrow Neck there could be no doubt at all. Now, however, it was not merely a question of opening an outlet in a convenient place, but of planning a series of main channels which would have the effect of draining the whole face of the country. Sceptics and croakers pooh-poohed the thing as an absurdity. It was declared the country was so flat that a drain would have to be made every 20 yards to get rid of the water. Others averred that, drain as much as you pleased, underground springs would flood the country when all the rainfall was disposed of. And certainly there were difficulties enough in the way to make the whole success of the work depend upon accurate knowledge and good judgment in determining the course and capacity of the drains to be constructed. But Mr. Goyder has proved himself fully equal to the responsibility he undertook, and he can now point to actual results to refute adverse predictions and justify his own action. His first course was to employ a strong staff of surveyors to take the levels of the whole of the country that was subject to inundation. This has now been completed so far as the most important section of the work is concerned, although it was not necessary to wait for all the levels before proceeding with the works at the extreme southern end of the wet country. It was evident that

---

* Pages 8 and 9.

† The Hon. William Milne, to whom I have already referred as the first Minister to authorize and earnestly support the Drainage Works, is also entitled to the credit of placing them under Mr. Goyder's control. When Mr. Milne first visited the district in 1863, and became impressed with the feasibility and utility of draining the flats, he held office as Commissioner of Public Works. Subsequently when, in another Ministry, he became Commissioner of Crown Lands, recognising the value of Mr. Goyder's thorough knowledge of the subject, and of his practical and untiring energy, he caused the works which he had previously sanctioned as Minister of Public Works to be transferred from that department, and Mr. Goyder was thereupon entrusted. with the execution of the entire enterprise.

other cuttings would have to be made in the ridge south of the Narrow Neck, rather than attempt to concentrate all the southern waters at that point, and accordingly two favorable positions were selected, and contracts for the work let in the early part of 1867. These were the cuttings now known as Milne's Gap and English's Gap respectively, and the discretion displayed in their selection has been amply verified. Another one has yet to be made near the German Creek to tap the waters of the German swamp which, with the exception of the comparatively small swamp near Port MacDonnell, presents what I may call the southern boundary of the wet country. Concurrently with the opening of Milne's Gap and English's Gap, the contract for which was taken by Mr. James Mackenzie, Mr. Goyder set a considerable number of men to work in extending the Narrow Neck cutting, and excavating drains leading from it, and also from the other gaps. The depth of the 8 chains of cutting at the Neck was increased to from 6 to 11 feet, and its width to 54 feet, with a further cutting to a width of 90 feet on the foot of the ridge, for the purpose of breaking the force of the water before it passed through the piers of the bridge which it had been necessary to construct.

When these three openings in the Woakwine range were completed no time was lost in pushing on with the main drains, which had been by this time adopted. It must be premised, however, that the completion of the levelling of the country indicated a more favorable fall and greater saving in cutting than was originally expected, and consequently there has been some alteration in the first projected course of the drains, and a corresponding increase in efficiency and economy.

We will make a start now at the Narrow Neck, and, if the reader will refer to the map, it will be found clearly indicated as about the slightest portion of the range, just cutting off the Cootel Swamp from Lake Frome, and within three miles of Greytown, Rivoli Bay, of which more anon. I have already given the present dimensions of the cutting at the Neck, and it will be understood that the water which escapes there spreads over the flat on the margin of Lake Frome, and finds its way thence into the Lake itself. As I go on I shall indicate the fall which has been obtained by stating the levels at certain points along the lines of drains, and it will be seen therefrom that there is a regular and quite sufficient increase of altitude to the eastward. For instance, Lake Frome, lying between the coast ridge and the Woakwine range, of which the "Neck" is a part, is 2·5 feet above the level of the sea, whereas the bottom of the Neck cutting is 21 feet above the level on the Lake side, and 26 feet above the level on the swamp or inland side of the range. Just at that point — the fall of the range on the inland side — a singular deposit of flints has been discovered in the excavations for the cutting, which have probably formed the bed of an ancient river. The deposit is about forty feet wide, resting on a bed of clay six feet below the surface, and all the stones are evidently water-worn. Nowhere else in the vicinity have flints been found, and the course of this phenomenon would really justify the geological assumption that a river rippled peacefully on its way there before the upheaval of the range dissipated its existence. From the Neck cutting a drain 40 feet wide is carried across the Cootel Swamp for a distance of a mile, where it enters a lower or western section of the Mount Muirhead flat, and where also a branch drain diverges on a line a point or two north of east to a gap in the Belt Range at the Calcolat Creek, and then turns on a sharp curve to the south, tapping the waters which accumulate on the eastern or inland side of that range. This, indeed, is one of the clearly defined conditions of all the flats of the district, which the reader should thoroughly understand. As I have so frequently pointed out, all the ranges run in parallel lines from south-east to north-west, the flats lying between them having a regularly increasing rise to the eastward. Thus there is always an accumulation of water on the western side of the flat where its fall is intercepted by the dividing range. Travellers by the mail will, I am sure, have noticed this circumstance even between Kingston and Narracoorte, and so uniform is the configuration of the district that exactly the same thing occurs as far south as the wet flats extend. The Belt range, which the branch drain I am referring to crosses, is only some eight miles long, lying about equi-distant between the main Woakwine and Reedy Creek Ranges, in the very centre of the Mount Muirhead flat, but in every other respect except its isolation it is identical in character, and in its course, so far as it goes, with the other ridges. The bottom of this branch drain at Calcolat Creek, where it crosses the Belt, is 32 feet above the sea level, so that even from that point to the junction with the main drain there is a fall of four feet, the bottom of the main drain there being 28 feet above the level.

From this junction the main drain swerves slightly to the south of east for about six miles, where it heads the southern end of the Belt Range, and then turning again to the north of east crosses the Mount Muirhead flat, tapping the Poolna Springs at the foot of Mount Muirhead, and continuing to the southern head of the Reedy Creek Range, exactly northwest of and about a mile distant from Mount Graham. At this point it will receive the lower waters that now flow to the Reedy Creek from the south and flood the Avenue flat, and from thence it will cross the Mount Graham flats on a slight curve to the southward round Campbell's Hill, about two miles due east of which there will be another and the last divergence, the one branch thence running on a north-easterly line direct to within two or three miles south of Penola, and the other on a south-easterly line past the extinct craters of Lake Leake and Lake Edward to the Dismal Swamp, which it will tap two miles south of Tarpeena. Both of these branches will pass through a considerable area of purchased land in the Hundreds of Young, Grey, and Penola, but I imagine the owners of it will be glad to allow any liberties of that kind to be taken with their freeholds in view of the substantial benefits they will be ensured by the work. On the other hand no one would wish to see the reclamation of the Dismal Swamp sacrificed because to effect it will necessarily be to benefit some fortunate land owners by the way. I will give the levels of the Dismal and Penola, to show how good a fall will be obtained for the drainage of the immense bodies of water that will be tapped by these extensions. The surface water of the Dismal is 213 feet above the sea level where the drain will tap it on the boundary of Mingbool, and 225 feet where it is intersected by the Penola new road. The point where the branch drain to Penola will terminate is 191·8 above the sea level. Beyond a certain point on the eastward there is a fall from the Dismal to the Glenelg, but that will not affect the drain which will tap the swamp on the borders of the Mingbool Hundred, although advantage will probably be taken of it to complete the drainage of the eastward section of the swamp. I shall defer saying anything about the quality of the country through which these drains will pass until I have indicated the course of the other drains leading to Milne's Gap and English's Gap, which, with the German Creek Drain, will complete the reclamation of all the flats on the south end of the district. And it must be understood that although I have spoken of the drains diverging from near Campbell's Hill to Penola and to the Dismal Swamp as branches, they will be in character and capacity essentially "main" lines. From the Narrow Neck to the first junction on the Mount Muirhead Flat, the main trunk drain will be as I have said, 40 feet wide; thence onward to the Campbell's Hill Junction the same width or nearly so will be preserved, and the branches from that point will be 30 feet wide. Originally it was intended to take the trunk line through the Belt Range at Calcolat Creek to the Reedy Creek waters, in which case what is now the continuation of the main line would have been only a branch terminating at the south end of the Belt. It was in fact only cut to a width of 20 feet in the first instance, but it will now have to be extended, as the trunk line, to the width I have mentioned. The alteration was adopted because it was found when all the levels were obtained that by taking that course the double object of draining the Penola country and the Dismal Swamp could be achieved, with about 10 miles less of main drain than was at first designed.

Following the course of the Woakwine range south-easterly, or parallel with the coast, from the Narrow Neck it preserves—

excepting on the approach to the Mayurra Station, where it expands considerably— a uniform width of from a mile to a mile and a half to its termination at the German Swamp, a distance of about 18 miles. At the two points where Milne's and English's Gaps have been cut it is narrowed, as at the Neck, by indentations which have been in the past mere swamp basins, accumulating a wealth of deposit that will now be utilised. Milne's Gap is 10 miles, English's Gap 13 miles, and the German Creek cutting about 15 miles south of the Narrow Neck. All of these gaps will give the waters, which have hitherto been dammed back by the range, outlets to Lake Bonney which has in its turn an outlet at its southern extremity to the sea. Between the lake and the range there is a flat nearly a mile wide, which bears a vast deposit of black vegetable soil. Now, like the flat on the margin of Lake Frome, it is considerably flooded by the drainage waters, but even it will be eventually capable of reclamation by the extension of the drains from the gaps in the ridge into the lake. There is quite a sufficient fall for the purpose, the water in Lake Bonney being only two feet above the sea level, whereas the bottom of the cutting at Milne's Gap is 27 feet higher. It is not proposed to go on with these extensions until the higher levels have been drained, but the value of the whole scheme may be inferred even from this instance of its simplicity and effectiveness.

The cutting through the ridge at Milne's Gap is 858 feet long, and its greatest depth, measuring from the highest point of the ridge on the course of the cutting, is 28 feet. Originally it had a width of five feet on the bottom, with a slope of one in one, but it was calculated that the effect of the scour through it would be to increase that width materially. This has already been realised. The soil on the surface is of the same character as that which prevails on the ridge—a light brown loam, intermixed with a good deal of shell limestone, more or less decomposed. But at only a few feet below the surface there is nothing but shell sand or shell sandstone. At first sight it would appear to be pure quartz sand, hardened here and there to stone, but a closer examination will show that the minute particles are shells. Take up a handful of sand and you grasp millions of distinctly formed shells ; or crumble a piece of the rock, which you may do easily with your fingers, and you have the same result. It will be easily understood that an immense body of water pouring constantly through a narrow cutting like this, with a velocity of four miles an hour, will very soon and effectively undermine walls of such material, and sweep away the debris in its course. This is just what it was expected to do, and what to a great extent it has done, even before the full force of the scour has been obtained. Slowly, but irresistibly, the running water eats its way into the mass of shell, and gradually, but helplessly, the upper strata thus undermined tumbles into the stream to be swept onward with the flood, and spread over the flat lying between the ridge and Lake Bonney. A better qualification of the too rich vegetable deposit there could hardly be desired, and it will be vastly finer for the admixture when it is reclaimed in its turn. Already by this means the bottom of the cutting has been increased from five feet to ten feet. It is expected that width will at least be doubled in another year, and a considerable width of the surface soil has been cleared of timber on each side, so as to

prevent anything falling into the drain that might obstruct the free course of the water. From the Gap a main drain 30 feet wide extends for nearly a mile through the swamp, and then turns sharply to the north-west for a mile and a half, and then again to the north-east for a mile, through a low narrow bank into the Wyrie Swamp, which it crosses still on a north-easterly line to another low ridge, which separates the swamp from the Mount Muirhead Flat. The Wyrie Swamp is about two and a half miles wide by nearly four miles long, and has heretofore been almost useless for any purpose ; but when the drainage is completed it will be one of the richest spots reclaimed. The ridge which encloses it is about half a mile wide where the drain crosses it to the Mount Muirhead Flat. Up to that point, i.e., the ridge on its eastern side, the drain from Milne's Gap has been cut by the Government party under Mr. Charles Bütte, a skilful engineer and a thoroughly practical man, to whom the local superintendence of the whole of the works has been entrusted by Mr. Goyder. The surface of the Wyrie Swamp is 40 feet, and the bottom of the drain 36·9 feet above the level of the sea, showing a fall of more than 7 feet to Milne's Gap. On the Mount Muirhead Flat side of the ridge, where the drain diverges, the surface of the ground is 46 feet, and the bottom of the drain 40 feet above the sea level, still showing an ample fall in figures, which has been abundantly verified in practice. The contract for the cutting through this eastern bank of the Wyrie Swamp and of the drains which diverge from it, which I will presently define, was originally taken and partly executed by Mr. McKenzie, who had previously carried out the contract for Milne's and English's Gaps, the Mount Gambier Hospital, and some other works in the South-

East. He was, however, compelled to relinquish the work, and in the first half of the present year the completion of the contract was undertaken by Mr. Dalwood. At the point where the drain reaches the Mount Muirhead Flat, the levels of which are given above, the divergence occurs, the one line following down the western side of the ridge for nearly five miles on a south-easterly line to the Nangula Springs, and the other crossing the flat a little north of east for about two and a half miles to the Teatree Springs, one and a half miles south of Mount Muirhead. Up to this junction the main drain from Milne's Gap preserves a uniform width of 30 feet, but each of the branches gradually diminishes to its termination at the point named. At the Nangula Springs, where the south-eastern branch ends, the surface is 48 feet and the bottom of the drain 43 feet above the sea level, and at the Teatrees near Mount Muirhead, the surface has an elevation of 52 feet, and the bottom of the drain of 44·5 feet. Those are all the drains that will be connected with Milne's Gap, but they will tap large bodies of water, and be—or, I may say, they already are—exceedingly effective in their operation.

English's Gap is a cutting through the ridge, three miles south of Milne's Gap, 561 feet in length, 33 feet from the bottom to the highest point of the ridge, and was five feet wide on the bottom originally. The work was precisely the same as at Milne's Gap, and the same widening process is going on by scouring, although in a less degree, because the body of water passing through there is also much less ; but that will be considerably increased when the leading drains are finished. From this Gap a main drain intersects the adjacent swamp extending about a mile slightly north of east, where there

is a low ridge cutting off the German Swamp waters. The drain is continued through this ridge, from whence one branch turns sharp to the south-east for a couple of miles, and another goes on north of east for about three miles through a wet honeysuckle flat, terminating a mile and a-half south of the Nangula Springs, and tapping a large extent of swamp on the north-east corner of the Hundred of Hindmarsh. The drain from the German Creek cutting will only extend some two to three miles, tapping the German swamp about a mile south of the south-eastern branch of the English's Gap drain.

These, then, are the whole of the works to be carried out to complete the drainage of the southern end of the district. They will of course materially affect all the wet country, even to its northernmost point, by intercepting and consequently reducing the vast bodies of water which formerly flooded it from the south. But the extent of country they will absolutely reclaim and render available for permanent occupation may be defined by the northern boundary line of the County of Grey, which extends, from Lake St. Clair on the coast due east to the Victorian border, passing about four miles north of Penola. Immediately north of that line in the County of Robe about 250 square miles comprising large portions of the Reedy Creek and Avenue Flats will be materially improved for grazing purposes, but other drains will be necessary there to completely reclaim that country. But omitting that extent from the calculation altogether, and confining ourselves to the County of Grey, we have a total area of 895 square miles to be absolutely reclaimed by the works actually in progress, and which I have already described. Of this extent 155 square miles, equal to 99,200 acres, are purchased in the Hundreds of Penola, Grey, Hindmarsh, and Young, and the balance of 740 square miles, or say, in round numbers, *half a million acres*, will be absolutely gained to the public estate, and to the beneficial resources of the colony, by the enterprise in progress.

Now, it would be absurd to ignore the fact that there is in the district, amongst certain sections of its population, a very positive prejudice against this work. It interferes with the good old order of things which elevated the sheepfarmers and stockholders of the "South-East" into territorial nabobs, and ensured them a comfortable monopoly for a nominal consideration. As long as those rich black flats were flooded long enough in the year to keep surveyors and buyers at a respectful distance, all was well. There was plenty of grass on the ridges in winter, and on the flats in summer, and water always. But when the fiat of reclamation went forth the serenity of monopoly was disturbed, and a host of objections found hasty and inconsiderate utterance. The climate would be ruined, said one, for there would be no stagnant water to attract the rain clouds—forgetful of course that when the rains commence to fill the swamps and flood the flats, is just the time when the surface ground is always dry. Then it was said the soil would be worthless when drained—it was either too rich or too poor, they weren't quite sure which; there is a bed of solid limestone within an inch of the surface, said one; if you break through the top crust of that swamp you'll go out of sight below, exclaimed another; you'll never get the water off that flat, said a third; and then some one else would echo, if you go cutting drains about there, and drop a lighted match on it, the whole flat will burn like tinder; and so on, until at last a very worthy gentleman and excellent sportsman capped the climax by entering an earnest and vigorous protest against the whole scheme, because "the confounded drainage would spoil the best snipe shooting in the country!" Really I am not sure that I shall not have to concede the point about the snipe shooting; although, after all, perhaps the Government might in the plenitude of their "reclaimed" wealth "preserve" a swamp or two, and construct a decoy pond, for the especial benefit of distressed sportsmen! But for the rest of these objections, as they raise questions affecting the climate, the character of the soil, and the efficiency of drains, they will be best answered by what I have still to say descriptively under each of those heads.

The efficiency of the drains to accomplish their intended purpose is certainly the most important question to be considered in connection with the whole scheme. I am glad, therefore, that the circumstance of my not having written this book with inconsiderate haste enables me to state now proved facts which place that question beyond dispute. If I had attempted to complete my report upon the works (and their results) when I first saw them a year and a half ago, I must necessarily have taken a good deal for granted which was then only conjecture or theory, but has now been realised practically. I have already stated the levels at various points along all the drains which are at present in progress, and it will be seen that they indicate a regular and sufficient fall throughout from the highest lying waters at Penola and the Dismal to the sea. And as far as any of the drains have been cut, the constant flow of water to the various outlets they lead to proves the certain existence of that fall. All that can be doubted, therefore, is whether the cuttings through the ridges and the drains leading thereto are of sufficient capacity to carry off the greatest accumulation of water which could result from the maximum rainfall upon the country they affect. The average rainfall of the district is 34 inches in the year, but in a thunderstorm as much as an inch and a half has fallen in an hour. The width of the drains has been calculated, not according to the average, but the maximum fall, and without any deduction for either the considerable absorption or evaporation which takes place; so that, as far as figures and calculations go, the capacity of the drains to meet any demand upon them is quite sufficiently established. But the objectors I have alluded to say—ah, but wait till we have a succession of the wet seasons that prevailed some years ago, and all your unfortunate settlers upon these flats will be flooded out. Indeed, one ingenious friend of mine once very pathetically assured me that even the top soil of the flats would inevitably be washed away through the gaps which had been so recklessly and foolishly cut through the ridges. But all these prejudiced people overlook the fact that the regular but very gentle fall to the seaboard—upon which at other times they insist—must entirely preclude a great rush of water except in the defined channels, unless as the result of an accumulation which when all the old barriers are cut through, and the drains are open throughout their course, can never possibly occur. Formerly the vast bodies of water which flooded the flat lands of the South-East resulted from the interruption of the natural fall by the ridges through which free courses are now secured, but for the future the waters, instead of being dammed back and accumulating, will flow on uninterruptedly in the channels constructed for their reception and escape. But if still more convincing evidence of capacity and efficiency is wanted, it has been already obtained, and as I witnessed it for myself, I may be excused for stating it positively. I must refer the reader to the description I have given of the drain cut from Milne's Gap through the Wyrie Swamp, and thence through the dividing ridge to the Mount Muirhead Flat, with its branches from that ridge to the Nangula Springs and the Teatree Springs respectively. The contractors for those two branch drains, and the ridge cutting to the Wyrie, very imprudently commenced the soft spade and shovel work on the flat before securing a means of egress for the water by completing the gap through the ridge. The natural and inevitable consequence was that when the rains set in (in June) the drains on the flat brought down vast quantities of water to the ridge, and being dammed back there it flooded out the cutting works which had just then been commenced. It therefore became necessary to erect heavy dams across both branch drains to enable the works on the ridge to proceed. Of course the result of this was a vast accumulation of water on the flat, far greater indeed than any that could possibly occur without the erection of artificial dams. Immediately behind the dam the depth was as much as seven feet, and the back water therefrom extended for miles upon the flat. Certainly such an accumulation could never have occurred there before, and never will again. Well, when at last the cutting through the ridge was completed, the dams were let go and the escape of this vast accumulation commenced. If the drain had then been unequal to sustain even so unusual and excessive a test the water must necessarily have overflown the banks and carried away the embankments. But although the drain further on through the Wyrie Swamp and up to Milne's Gap had not been cut to its full width of 30 feet, within 24 hours of the time when the dams were let go the Mount Muirhead Flat was perfectly dry where there had been, as the consequence of the dams, so great an accumulation. Then as to the efficiency of Milne's Gap, it was ascertained by actual measurement that, in the 24 hours following the breaking away of these dams, a body of water equal to double the extreme capacity of the Adelaide reservoir flowed through that cutting with a velocity of nearly four miles an hour. The fact of so vast a quantity of pent-up water being effectually drained away, and upwards of 250,000,000 gallons actually escaping through one cutting in 24 hours, even before the drain leading to it was excavated to its destined width, ought surely to convince the most sceptical that the efficiency of these drains may be relied upon. Another circumstance I was able to note from actual observation proves with equal clearness the accuracy of the stated levels, and the correct positions of the drains. The branch drain from the point where the dams I have been referring to were constructed, crossing the Mount Muirhead Flat a little north of east, directly intercepts the natural fall from the south-east, which is again intercepted by the main drain to the Narrow Neck on a parallel line two miles further north-west. The fall being invariably from east and south to west and north, the stuff taken out of the drains is of course embanked on their north sides. But in order to relieve the pressure upon the dams the embankment which had been already formed along this branch drain across the flat was cut through at several places, and the necessary result

was to flood the flat on the north-west of the drain with water from the south-east, which would otherwise have been intercepted and carried off by that channel. Here again was a greater accumulation than could possibly occur from ordinary causes, but the natural fall to the north-west was quite sufficient to drain away even that overflow to the main parallel channel, and within 24 hours from the drains being cut away it had all disappeared. Many other instances of equal significance might be given to the same effect, for indeed everywhere, as far as the drains have been completed, their thorough efficiency has been already amply demonstrated.

The next question to be considered is, the quality of the soil reclaimed. I have placed it second in order of importance, because even if the land were as bad as some of its prejudiced detractors allege it to be it would be improved, if not "reclaimed," by a thorough system of drainage. Therefore, I take it, our first business should be to test the efficiency of the drainage scheme, so far as getting rid of surplus water is concerned, and then to consider the value of the improvement effected, which must of course be measured by the character of the soil operated upon. I have already stated the extent of the wet land in the County of Grey that will be drained, and although it differs materially in quality from a large extent of the flats on the more northern and eastern levels of the district, the bulk of the half million acres affected by the present works is very uniform in character if not in actual value. It may seem paradoxical to imply that its character is equal and its value unequal, but the distinction is easily explained. Whatever difference there may be in the soil upon these flats is not so much in character as in development: the process of formation has been in fact the same, or pretty nearly so, throughout; but that formation is now, in various localities, presented in widely varying conditions of luxuriance and stages of maturity. This will be best understood by a simple statement of what the formation has been; and that may be expressed as the continual deposit of decaying vegetation and decaying shell upon a bed of shell-sand, marl, and pipeclay. And, if we admit the geological theory of upheaval as the true explanation of the apparent encroaches upon the coast lines of former ages, we can easily understand also why upon the higher and necessarily older terraces receding from the seaboard the formation is more advanced and complete, and the vegetable deposit less luxuriant than on the more modern levels nearer the present coast line. A further illustration of what, however promoted, has evidently been the process of formation may be obtained from the contrast of the swamp bottoms, resulting from occasional hollows or depressions upon the prevailing level, with the flats immediately adjacent to them. On the hollows where water has stood permanently vegetation has been coarse, consisting almost entirely of rushes and reeds, and cattle have been unable to do more than pick over the tops when green. There has thus been in such places a vast deposit of decaying vegetation accumulating year by year, not consolidated, as on the flats, by trampling down, and presenting now for a great depth a loose spongy mass of absolute manure with a slight admixture of actually formed soil. The roots of the rushes alone constitute a large proportion of the deposit, but a remarkable peculiarity of the formation is the plentiful addition of lime to the vegetable which

prevails in a greater or less degree on all the wet lands, and which results from a very simple but self-evident cause. A small shellfish, rarely exceeding half an inch in length, is found over the whole extent of the wet lands adhering to the rushes on the hollows and to the grass on the flats, and so numerous are these minute Testacea as to reduce the black soil, on which they ultimately fall and decay, to veritable grey in appearance. From the decomposition of these shells lime of course results, and hence arises what will be found in the future one of the most valuable characteristics of these reclaimed lands. The experience of the reclamation of peat bogs and other vegetable deposits from inundation in England and Ireland has proved the necessity there of adding lime as a manure, but certainly no such qualification will be required here. Although, by the way, I have alluded to these small shellfish as Testacea, I am not, I should confess, sufficiently versed in the science of conchology to determine whether they really belong to the testaceous or crustaceous order; but at any rate, the main difference between the two, so far as their effect upon the soil is concerned, would be simply that testaceous shells comprise only carbonate of lime and gelatinous matter, whereas crustaceous shells have, besides those elements, a small proportion of phosphate of lime. And even the superficial observer can hardly fail to be struck with the confirmation of geological theories propounded before Australia was explored, which is afforded by the constant prevalence throughout the South-Eastern district of limestone and shell in various stages of stratification or decay. The vast mountains of calcareous earth which occur in different parts of the world have been attributed to the decay of huge accumulations of marine testaceous animals, and certainly the geology of our South-Eastern district goes entirely to sustain the supposition.

It will be seen, then, that the component parts of the surface soils of all these reclaimed flats and swamps are simply decomposed vegetable and lime. The subsoil almost invariably consists of these same minute shells, intermixed with a whitish looking sticky sort of marl, but the depth of the vegetable deposit resting upon it varies considerably. The greatest accumulation is upon the hollows or swamp bottoms I have alluded to, such, for instance, as the Cootel and Wyrie Swamps. In the former of these, where the drain has been cut through to the Narrow Neck, there is a depth of 10 or 11 feet of vegetable deposit before you reach the calcareous bottom, and there, too, overlying that, is a bed of seaweed still undecayed, but perfectly purged of the saline character it must have possessed before it was wrested from the ocean by the upheaval of the Woakwine range. So long as the water remained upon those swamps permanently the vegetable deposit went on increasing without either consolidation or perfect decomposition, because it was impossible to graze down or even compress the excessive growth there. The nearest approach elsewhere to this prolific deposit is found invariably on the western sides of the flats, just under the ridges where the water has lain longer and in greater quantity, but on the general surfaces of the flats, which even before a drain was cut were dry during fully six months of the year, vegetation was less abundant, but more useful, and as the result of constant grazing and consolidation, the top soil, although shallower, is more advanced in formation, and certainly of greater immediate value. In fact on all the swamp bottoms, as distinguished from the flats, even where the water has been got rid of, cultivation will be impossible for the present. Ultimately they will become the richest spots, and in the meantime they will afford rare grazing areas, as finer grasses replace the coarse vegetation they have hitherto borne. There is one peculiarity of the black vegetable soil of these lower lying flats, where the surface is freer from sand than on the higher plateaus, or nearer the stringy bark ridges, which it is important to notice, and that is its extreme susceptibility to, and capacity to absorb and retain, moisture. Some persons have asserted that when the flats were drained vegetation would perish for want of moisture. But there is about as much probability of that as of sponge becoming non-absorbent. I have handled the soil when it has been in appearance as much like black snuff or gunpowder as anything, but when the least contact with wet would immediately convert it into a soapy sort of paste with all the retentiveness of clay without its pitch-like tenacity. Others again have declared that the bed of shell below the vegetable surface soil is so porous that water would run through it like a sieve. But there is so large a proportion of marl intermixed with the shell that it too is quite capable of retaining sufficient moisture for all purposes of vegetation. Of course these adverse allegations I am combating, and the many others I have previously exposed, are intended as so many bogies to scare away the agricultural settler, but I have no fear that they will accomplish any such mischievous result. Indeed as to the question of moisture, over all these flats the natural level of the springs is so near the surface that the drains are far more likely to do additional good service in relieving the subsoil, especially on the lower levels, of superabundant water than to destroy vegetation by abstracting all moisture from the surface.

The foregoing descriptions of the reclaimed land will apply more particularly to the section lying between the Woakwine and Reedy Creek Ranges, and extending from German Creek on the south to beyond the county boundary on the north, and the upper or southern end of which is known generally as the Mount Muirhead Flat. This, reckoning all the flat from German Creek to the Woakwine Swamp on the Northern extremity of the Belt Range, may be estimated as comprising upwards of 200 square miles of the best soil reclaimed, with a much larger area on the same flat—I mean between the same ranges — extending northward from the Woakwine. But on the eastern side of the Reedy Creek Range, commencing with the Mount Graham Flats on the south and going northward towards the Avenue Flat, the soil is not so rich, except in patches or under the range on its eastern side. It is for the most part lighter and sandier on the surface, and there is a less depth of vegetable deposit, owing I imagine to there having been a less luxuriant growth there. A large extent of the Mount Graham Flats, as well as of the wet heathy country lying between them and Penola, may be excepted from the area likely to become available as first-class agricultural land, although it will be vastly improved for grazing purposes ; but approaching Penola again, as well as about Kalangadoo and Tarpeena, there are some rich patches. On the Dismal, which is rather a series of isolated lagoons than an uninterrupted swamp, there are also some very rich spots varied by patches of poorer and shallower soil. Summarising, then, the whole extent of the reclaimed land in the County of Grey

alone, amounting it will be remembered exclusive of nearly 100,000 alienated acres, to *half a million acres* Crown lands, it may be concluded that the larger half of that area, or say upwards of 300,000 acres, is of the maximum degree of richness, and will be available for beneficial agricultural occupation. A large proportion of the remaining 200,000 acres, although inferior in quality and shallower in depth, will be also available for farming, or what is not will become exceedingly good grazing land. And it will bear repeating that these results will be obtained within the boundaries of the County of Grey ! A much larger extent of wet country— although perhaps scarcely so rich as the Mount Muirhead flat—will be reclaimed by future works in the Counties of Robe and Macdonnell. Of this more anon.

Following, in order of importance, the questions of the efficiency of the drains and the quality of the soil, we must next consider what are the facilities, existing or obtainable, for settlement, traffic, and export upon these large areas of reclaimed land. And upon the very threshold of this argument I have to encounter one more, and I think the last, of the many but misty objections which have been taken to the drainage scheme. It has been put to me thus—"Well, suppose these flats are effectually drained, and suppose the soil is as good as you say it is, where are the poor devils who buy it going to live ? Are they to build their homesteads upon piles ?" Of course if it were impossible to give a reasonable answer to such questions they would acquire some little importance, because artificial sites for homesteads, whether obtained upon a superstructure of piles or surrounded by necessary embankments, are not at all desirable. But the fact is Nature, in the plenitude of her wisdom, has silenced the objections of cavillers, and supplied the requirements of future settlers in a far more convenient and comfortable manner than any mere artist could design. It may be said to be a prevailing feature of the flats that wherever they exceed one or two miles in width between the ridges they are thickly studded with "islands," as I may call them, varying from one or two to one or two hundred acres in extent. These islands are of precisely the same character as the adjacent ridges, except, perhaps, that their elevation is not always so great. But they have the same description of soil—a light red loam, intermixed with shell sandstone or limestone — and the same varieties of timber—chiefly sheaoak and honeysuckle—as are found on the ridges. There are also gums and blackwood scattered about, so that stone for building, and wood for either building, fencing, or domestic purposes can be easily obtained. Of course, where it is practicable, a slice of the nearest ridge will be included in each surveyed section of reclaimed land, and wherever that cannot be conveniently managed the islands are as available and valuable for the purpose as if they had been placed there expressly to promote it. These, then, will be the homestead sites—either the ridges, the positions and character of which I have repeatedly described, or the patches of dry elevated ground of a similar description which, although isolated, are sufficiently numerous on the widest portion of the flats.

It will be admitted that wherever we have alternate strips of rich and inferior country, one material advantage resulting from the settlement of the good land is the greater value thereby given to the poorer land adjoining it. This will be especially realised in the settlement of these reclaimed areas. So long as the flats were subject to yearly inundation, and consequently valueless to the farmer, the narrow ridges intersecting them, in themselves too stony to be ploughed, could only possess a nominal because uncontested value to the State, derived of course from the graziers who monopolised them. But with the settlement of the reclaimed flats not only will the ridges become extremely valuable as homestead sites, but as grazing areas to be held on lease by the agricultural settlers there, in blocks proportioned to their freeholds. A concession of this kind, by which every bona fide purchaser for purposes of settlement of a section on the flats will acquire therewith a pre-emptive right to the grazing lease of a proportionate area of the stony but well-grassed land on the ridges, will be absolutely necessary to the perfect success of the work that is going on, and will besides have the advantage of securing to the State a material but equitable revenue from lands that under any other circumstances would remain comparatively worthless, or yielding very little more value, both to the State and to the occupier, than at present.

Another thing to be considered is the facilities available for fencing sections on the flats. If it were necessarily a question of post and rail or stone fences, there would be considerable difficulty and expense involved, as all the material would have to be carted from the ridges or islands. But this is a matter which may be dealt with in intimate conjunction with the very important question of obtaining free drainage from the entire surface of the flats to the main channels which intersect the ground. Under ordinary circumstances when a settler takes up a section his first business is to fence it in. But, in dealing with these wet lands, instead of erecting a fence the settler will have to dig a ditch round his property, and an open communication will have to be maintained between all these sectional ditches and the nearest main drain towards which they will fall. The stuff taken out of them will form embankments, which, if planted with quickset, or some other appropriate bush, will together give the hedge, bank, and ditch so familiar to English farmers, and which constitute half the beauty of rural scenery in the old country. They will effectively replace, and at a less cost, the dismal post-and-rail or wire fences which disfigure almost all Australian landscapes, and they will besides perfect the drainage of the country, and the consequent reclamation of the land. Obviously such subsidiary channels connecting with the main drains will be necessary to carry off the surplus water from the land on which it falls, and to intercept the drainage from sections lying higher. And if in ploughing the lands care is taken to leave open stetch furrows and cross water furrows leading into the ditches, which in their turn will lead into the main drains, there will be nothing to fear from floods, or even from a waterlogged surface. After all, such precautions are no more than every farmer in England makes his every-day business, and they will be very soon understood and easily practised here.

I have shown now how the necessary requirements of homestead sites, grazing areas, sectional fencing, and complete surface drainage can all be readily and inexpensively supplied. But this is not all. It will be as easy, under the system which is being carried out, to irrigate lands adjacent to the drains as it is now to convey all the surplus water to the lakes or to the sea. At some times, and for some crops, irrigation will certainly be a valuable adjunct, if not an absolutely necessary precaution, and in order that it may be readily resorted to, sluice-gates will be erected at convenient places along all the drains. With all these resources at his command, and with incomparably rich soil to work upon, the settler upon these flats can hardly fail in his enterprise if he brings ordinary intelligence and reasonable industry to bear upon it. He will have the choice of grain, pulse, or root crops, varied again with clovers or artificial grasses. He will be able to combine stock-keeping with husbandry, and to bring far more than ordinary advantages to bear upon both branches of his business; and finally, he will possess unusual facilities for the conveyance and export of his produce. Upon these last two questions I must say a few words specifically.

It would be quite possible, if it were desired to do so, to render all the main drains permanently navigable as canals. The depth to which they are already cut, ranging from five to six feet, taps the permanent level of the springs which abound throughout the district; and this source, combined with the drainage waters, would be sufficient, with the assistance of occasional locks, to keep a constant supply of water in the drains, and if they were deepened to about seven feet they might be navigated by punts or flat-bottomed barges. But apart from this, which it may not be expedient to effect at present, roads or light railways can be very easily constructed along the course of the drains. The stuff taken out of the channels is necessarily, as I have explained, embanked on the north side of all the cuttings, and thus the permanent bed upon which to make either a road or railway is already secured. If a metalled road is adopted, limestone for its construction can be obtained in abundance from the ridges; or, if a railway should be preferred, timber suitable for sleepers may be procured there also. Under any circumstances, bye-roads can be very easily and cheaply constructed along the branch drains. They would be exceedingly useful to the settlers there, and would be valuable as feeders for the main lines to Rivoli Bay. These latter would; of course, following the main drains, extend from the Dismal Swamp through the Tarpeena and Kalangadoo country; and from Penola, skirting Kalangadoo on a south-west line to the point of junction, near Mount Macintyre; and the main united line would follow thence past Mount Graham and Mount Muirhead direct to the Narrow Neck, which is only three miles from the south end of Rivoli Bay, where Grey Town, a Government township, was originally laid out. The distance by this route from Penola to the Narrow Neck would be 45, and from Tarpeena 40 miles. But inasmuch as it is generally conceded now that the north end of Rivoli Bay would afford a much better port than the south end, where the now-deserted township and port was declared many years ago, it would be necessary to carry the line for about nine miles along the Woakwine Range to near Johnson's Woakwine head station, from whence it would cross to the bay in about four miles further. I should by no means advocate the opening of a fourth port on the south-east coast if it were not that Rivoli Bay is so much nearer the best and largest extent of the reclaimed lands than any other already in existence or which it is possible to obtain. Neither is Rivoli Bay likely to become a first-class harbor. Its disadvantages are that at the south end, it is exposed to north winds, and at the north end to south winds; but of the two the north site is preferred, because it is somewhat

better sheltered and has deeper water. It is, therefore, almost to be accepted as a necessary result of the drainage enterprise that a new port should be established, a township laid out, and a jetty built at the north end of the bay, as an outlet for the produce that will soon be raised on the rich reclaimed lands in its immediate vicinity. When this is done, and either a tramway or road constructed along the embankments which border the main drains from the Dismal Swamp (with a terminus at Tarpeena) and from Penola, the settlers on the flats will certainly possess all the facilities for traffic and export which I have anticipated for them, and it will besides give the rapidly increasing agriculturists about Penola the choice of another outlet for their produce, which will probably be as acceptable to them as the proposed line thence to MacDonnell Bay. But it would be unadvisable to go further into this question until I come to the consideration of the requirements of the district as a whole.

A word or two about the ruins of Grey Town. I visited the deserted site of what was once a lively little seaport town, on a stormy day in June, when a strong north wind was blowing, which quite satisfied me that if I were master of a vessel I would rather be at the north end of the Bay—just then, at all events. Even in crossing Lake Frome, which is not much more than two miles wide, we had a good deal of tumbling about on the waters of that little landlocked basin. Three of us were cramped up in a diminutive flat-bottomed cockleshell of a boat, and as we sat there, wet, shivering, and stiff, I could not refrain from enquiring how deep it was to the bottom. But the gentleman who was my "guide, philosopher, and friend," on the occasion was admirably adapted to preserve jollity under adverse circumstances. I will not disclose his personality, but those who know him well will probably recognise his genial nature in the following impromptu, which ought not to be altogether lost. Our boatman, who was striving hard for headway with his oars, got into the habit of ducking his head to avoid the pretty constant shower-baths the waves favored us with, until at last my friend exclaimed in deep sonorous tones—"Ugh! never mind Smit (Smith), it is only de vater. I vish it vas de brandy!"

There is something very unpleasantly suggestive about the ruins of a deserted township in a young colony like this. Here was a new enterprise—the nucleus of what might have been, if only reasonably good judgment had been used, a thriving centre of commerce and export, useful in the past and trebly valuable now—consigned prematurely to the cold shade of desolation and decay. There are ample evidences left even now to testify to the industry that was wasted and the speculations that were ruined. I suppose the township to be declared at the other end of the Bay, where this should have been, will be called New Grey Town; but what is left of the old place will, let us hope, long retain its present isolated distinction as the ruins of the only absolutely abandoned settlement in South Australia. Even the city of Palmerston is jealously guarded and revered by Mira and his faithful followers, although its founders have deserted it; but not even a shepherd on any adjacent station deigns to honor the remains of Grey Town with his presence or his care. I read upon the walls of what was once a general store, kept by Mr. Crouch, of Mount Gambier, a variety of inscriptions which reveal what may be accepted, I suppose, as the history of the port since its abandonment; but their story is neither exciting nor remarkable. For instance one records that "The screw steamer Mullagh put into Rivoli Bay, August 20, 1856, for shelter in a gale of wind. –V. G. Denston, master." Another says; "The workmen for building a house for George Glen, Esq., at Mayurra, arrived here by the Kangaroo, 16th February, 1857, sixteen days out from Adelaide." There are a good many others to the same effect, but none of those numerous visitors seem to have liked the ruins well enough to stay there. Sic transit! I hope whoever else some years hence may undertake to write a description of the South-Eastern District will have a more cheerful story to relate of Rivoli Bay than mine has been.

There is one other important matter to be considered in connection with the drainage scheme, and it is the only one remaining for me to deal with. What will be the cost of the work? and what proportion will the cost bear to the results obtained? Fortunately the questions are capable of very simple and satisfactory solution. Up to the end of 1867 the total amount expended on the works, including those executed by the Government parties under Mr. Bütte as well as those contracted for, was £9,365 1s. In the present year (1868) the total amount expended has been £14,794 8s. 4d. To carry on the main drains to Penola and the Dismal Swamp, the course and effect of which I have described, and which will complete the drainage of the southern end of the district within the boundaries of County Grey, a further sum of £54,575 will be required, making a grand total of £78,734 9s. 4d., or say in round numbers £80,000. In return for this expenditure, the first material gain to the national estate will be the excess of the actual money value of the land absolutely reclaimed over the value it possessed in its normal state. Let us see what this may be computed at. Within County Grey, exclusive of about 100,000 acres of purchased land beneficially affected by the drains, the area of Crown Lands reclaimed will be about 740 square miles, or say in round numbers equal to 500,000 acres. As I have already shown, 300,000 acres of this area will be, in its reclaimed state, first-class agricultural land, and the remaining 200,000 acres fair agricultural or really good pastoral land: Estimating the value of the best at £2 10s. per acre—and there can be no doubt it will realise that, or more, when all the advantages it combines are understood—we may put down the 300,000 acres at £750,000 ; and if any one is sceptical about this estimate of £2 10s. per acre, let me remind him that it is less than one-fifth of the value—realised every day—of the best agricultural land at Mount Gambier. Then taking the 200,000 acres of second-class reclaimed land at only £1 10s. per acre, we may put down for that £350,000, or £1,100,000 for the half-million acres. Now let us see what return is obtained at present from that country, and deduct it. I have run through the recent valuations, now in force, on ten of the principal leases in the County of Grey, comprising the best of the wet lands in conjunction with the dry and finely-grassed ridges, and I find the valuated rental upon them averages £4 per mile, or three half-pence per acre. Capital derivable from the alienation of our landed estate, and applicable to reproductive public works, is worth 5 per cent. to the country, inasmuch as we borrow for those purposes at that rate. Consequently the annual money value derivable from the 500,000 acres of reclaimed land

would amount to £55,000, as against the rental it yields at present, taken at three half-pence per acre, of £3,125. Thus the excess of mere money value resulting from the drainage may be taken at £51,975 per annum, representing a clear gain in capital of £1,039,500 for an outlay of £80,000 !

But no reasonable man would measure the value of such an enterprise to the State merely by the increased revenue it returned directly to the National Treasury. A long list of collateral advantages might be enumerated, almost any one of which would afford in itself adequate compensation for the outlay that has been incurred. For instance, the greater value given to the intersecting ridges by the agricultural occupation of the reclaimed flats ; the conversion of what has hitherto been a comparative waste isolating the rich districts around Penola and Kalangadoo from the seaboard to a continuous area available for profitable settlement, as the result of which connection instead of isolation will be secured ; and the more than probable extinction of coast disease there by the dispersion of stagnant surface water. But a greater gain than all these will be realised in the expansion of the material wealth of the country which must result from the largely increased return, in produce, that will be extracted from these lands. Let us see how this aspect of the case presents itself. A sheep to two acres is certainly the extreme carrying capability of this country, even taking the ridges with the flats, in its unimproved condition. Seven and sixpence per head would be, I imagine, an ample estimate for wool and increase. If these calculations are correct—and I am afraid they are rather over the mark than under it—it would follow that the gross annual return per acre which these lands have yielded under sheep in the past must be taken at about 3s. 9d. Under agriculture we may fairly estimate the gross annual return, allowing either for rotation of crops or alternate cropping and grazing, at £2 per acre. Indeed £2 would be a reasonable estimate for the Adelaide Plains, but on the rich vegetable deposits of these flats, and with the larger rainfall which prevails there, a higher average might be fairly taken. But even at those figures—excessive probably as to the sheep and certainly moderate as to agriculture—the 500,000 acres would yield an annual return in gross money value of £93,750 in the one case as against £1,000,000 in the other. And even this is not all, for when the intersecting ridges which come now under the estimate of 3s. 9d. per acre, are enclosed in small grazing paddocks, and are worked in conjunction with farming operations on the flats, their carrying capabilities will certainly be increased. I know that in opposition to all this it will be said farming does not pay as well as squatting. Of course a farmer cannot realise so large a profit on an 80-acre section for which he pays, say £2 per acre, equal at 10 per cent. to £16 per annum, as a squatter can upon four square miles of country which he gets at the same annual cost. But certainly a larger aggregate profit would be realised upon these 500,000 acres under agriculture than would be possible under sheep, and it would be disseminated amongst 1,000 farmers, reckoning an average of 500 acre holdings, instead of being monopolised by half a score squatters, i.e., allowing, say 78 square miles to each. And, again, contrasting the £93,750, the gross return under sheep, with the £1,000,000, the gross return under agriculture, whatever proportion of the difference between the

two amounts does not represent an increase of net profit would be necessarily expended in the employment of additional labor, the interest upon additional capital invested, and the general charges of raising the produce. So that the power of the country to sustain a population, and the scope it affords for the remuneration of industry and the investment of capital must necessarily be increased in the same degree, to the certain promotion of our national prosperity and progress. It cannot be denied that the possibility of realising these advantages is entirely attributable to the drainage, for, until that had been undertaken and accomplished, agriculture could never have been introduced on those 500,000 acres at all. I think, therefore, I have proved the beneficial nature of the enterprise, and fully justified the assertion I have already made that the originators of the scheme, whoever they were—Mr. Milne, who was the first Minister of the Crown to recognise its importance and sanction its prosecution; Mr. Butte, who as Engineer in Charge under Mr. Goyder, has worked with great energy, self-denial, and zeal; and especially Mr. Goyder, with whom rests the entire credit of designing and successfully executing the work, as would the responsibility had he failed, are all fairly entitled to the gratitude of the people of South Australia for the grand results they have placed within our reach.

The contracts for the completion of the works I have been reviewing will be very soon ready to let. They will comprise the extension of the main drain from the Mount Muirhead Flat to near Mount Macintyre, and its branches thence to Penola and the Dismal. They will be offered in twenty sections, to be commenced simultaneously, by which means it is hoped the whole work may be absolutely finished and the entire series of drains and sluices placed in working order before the wet season of 1869 commences. Surveys will also be pushed on, and the first sales of the reclaimed lands will probably be announced about next April. In the meantime whatever else may be done for land reform, some special legislation will be necessary as to the terms on which these lands may be alienated, and as to the maintenance and regulation of the drains. Some useful hints as to the latter subject will, no doubt, be obtained by the Government from the system in force in Holland on the embanked low lands there; and as to sale, it will be a monstrous injustice to the colony if a single acre of the flats, capable of being profitably farmed, is alienated except under stringent conditions of occupation and cultivation. Speculating or pastoral monopolies must be absolutely forbidden there.

The extension of the drainage scheme to the wet lands to the north of those now being reclaimed, lying chiefly within Counties Robe and MacDonnell, will not be undertaken, at all events, until after the work at present in progress has been completed. The limits of the two schemes are clearly defined by the natural fall, for from a certain line north of Mount Muirhead the waters flow directly to the Reedy Creek from the Avenue Flats, and by that channel they escape to Salt Creek, and thence to the Coorong. The exact course which the drains that will lead into Reedy Creek will take, and the points at which gaps must be cut in the ridges, cannot, of course, be determined until levels have been taken on that country, as they have been already from the Woakwine Range to Penola and the Dismal. The area that will then have to be dealt with is much larger than that now being operated on; but there is a smaller pro-

portion of rich land to be reclaimed. Altogether, the northern drains having outlets from the Reedy Creek to Salt Creek and the Coorong, and from Maria Creek to the sea, will affect about 2,500 square miles, of which probably not more than 1,000 miles can be classed, when reclaimed, as really good agricultual land- The rest will, however, be rendered extremely valuable for pastoral purposes, almost or quite to the northern boundary of County MacDonnell. The best of these lands will be comprised in portions of the Biscuit and Avenue Flats, the Maria Creek Swamp, which I have described minutely in previous articles, and also in the swampy sections of Mosquito Plains. The latter, lying on the higher terraces to the eastward, are subject to comparatively little inundation beyond that arising from the rainfall upon them, and may be drained by smaller channels than are necessary on the lower levels.

Before finally concluding my notes of the Mount Muirhead District there are one or two features of the country there, and extending towards Mount Gambier and Penola, having no relation to the drainage works which claim a passing notice. Mount Muirhead itself, the western extremity of a spur of the range which extends on a north-west line from Mount Burr to the Reedy Creek, forms a prominent and somewhat remarkable object. Like most of the isolated eminences in the southern part of the district which are apparently of volcanic origin, it resembles in form a huge sugar loaf lying on its side, having a gradual rise to its highest point terminating in a sudden and almost precipitous fall. It is quite destitute of timber, and being of considerable height forms a conspicuous land mark from all parts of the flat to the coast; its plain but verdant surface presenting a strong contrast to the dismal hues of the scrubby timber at its foot. I took the trouble to ascend it, and from the summit, where a trig station has been established, a good view of the surrounding country may be obtained. The whole course of the flat, which takes its name from the Mount, may be plainly discerned, and beyond it on the west the Woakwine Range, then Lakes Bonney and Frome, then the coast sand ridge, and finally the sea. The soil on the Mount is good—a rich chocolate loam with limestone underlaying, and occasionally outcropping. It is the freehold property of Mr. A. Johnson, of Mount Graham, who purchased it many years ago, and it may be certainly considered one of the "eyes" of the country. It presents, too, a magnificent site for a township, and is almost certain to be availed of for that purpose when the progress of settlement on the flat necessitates that kind of accommodation.

I don't know that it would be possible to find anywhere in the colony a greater abundance of the various species of game common to Australia than prevails in the vicinity of this Mount. During a lengthened stay in its vicinity I scarcely ever passed it without seeing a flock of emus, or a mob of kangaroo, or both, on some part of it; and the ferns, which are dense and luxuriant everywhere on the lower and sandier slopes of the range, extending to Mount Graham and Mount Burr, fairly swarm with marsupials. From the diminutive "brush," not much bigger than a buck rabbit, to the lordly "old man," squatting six feet high on his hams and tail, the brutes live, increase, and flourish. On the flats wild turkeys are plentiful, and on the lagoons on the timbered flats stretching northward from the foot of Mount Graham wild duck, teal, geese, and swan abound at certain seasons of the year. Presently, when agricultural industry, the smoke of cities, and the shrill whistle of the locomotive shall have invaded these now almost unpeopled wilds, the emus and turkeys will disappear, and the kangaroo nuisance may possibly be reduced within reasonable limits; but the sportsman may find for the present endless attraction and constant incentives to enjoyment there. For sport, considered apart from the value of your bag, it would be difficult to find anything prettier in its way than brush kangaroo shooting in the ferns; and stalking an emu in the timber, or manœuvreing a turkey on the open flat, will sustain a lengthened tremor of that fascinating excitement which only the true sportsman knows.

Three miles north-east of Mount Muirhead, Mount Graham forms another conspicuous object in the range. Wider in extent and more gradual in elevation, if less distinctive in appearance, it is in other respects of more importance than Mount Muirhead. It presents on its summit and slopes a considerable area of good lightly timbered soil, the freehold of which was also secured years since by Mr. Johnson, whose hospitable residence and head station stand at a good elevation on its northern side, overlooking a wide extent of wet but wooded country, called, of course, the Mount Graham Flats, extending to the Avenue Flat on the north, and towards Penola on the north-east. Going thence direct to Penola, several belts of wet heathy country have to be crossed between the ranges, but by making a slight divergence to the eastward you may pass through the rich district of Kalangadoo, through which the surveyed, but unconstructed, line of tramway from Mount Gambier to Penola also goes. An idea of the value of the .

Kalangadoo land may be formed from the fact that years ago it realised as much as £3 per acre, and bona fide farmers who settled upon it then are doing well, and have comfortable homesteads upon moderately extensive freeholds. But a large extent of it has been purchased by squatters who keep it still under sheep. It is a rich black loam on the surface, easily worked and very productive. What may be called the Kalangadoo district lies chiefly within the Hundred of Grey, and almost all the hundred except its north-western corner has been alienated from the Crown.

From Mount Graham towards Mount Gambier the course lies along the foot of a stringybark range to Mount Burr, another very prominent landmark, on which also a trig station is established. A more extensive view may be obtained from its summit than from Mount Muirhead, the view towards the coast being the same, except that it is enlarged by the addition of the intervening country, and that a wide prospect, embracing Mount Gambier and Mount Schanck, is opened to the south-east, and Kalangadoo and the Penola heaths are visible to the north-east. I strongly recommend any traveller in the district, who wishes a good blow and a clear idea—as presented by a perfect birds'-eye view—of the lay of the country there, and the course of the drains, to ascend

Mount Burr. To do so he must leave the track a little at Grist's public-house where he will be sure to obtain the necessary directions. There is some good land, although limited in extent, on the higher slopes of the Mount, and there the boundary fences of the three principal runs in the vicinity—Mayurra, Mount Graham, and Glencoe—unite. About five miles from Mount Burr there are two considerable lakes, evidently extinct craters. They are included in the late Mr. Leake's purchases on Glencoe and are named respectively Leake and Edward. There is a small area of exceedingly good country around them, but beyond that again you have stringybark ridges towards Kalangadoo on one line, and almost to the Glencoe head-station on the other. A curious fact has been ascertained respecting these lakes in levelling the district for the drainage. Although they are only about half a mile apart, the level of the surface of the water in Lake Leake is exactly equal to the bottom of Lake Edward, the surface water of the former being 314 feet above the level of the sea, with a depth of 17 feet, and the surface of the latter 350 feet above the sea level, but with a depth of 37 feet. How this singular fact is to be accounted for is a nut I must leave to others to crack.

CHAPTER IX.

PENOLA: THE TOWNSHIP AND ADJACENT DISTRICT.

From Lake Leake Penola is distant 22 miles to the north-east, and Mount Gambier 19 miles to the south-east. I shall better preserve the continuity of these descriptions by dealing with the Penola country first, as I have already alluded to certain sections of it. In describing the Mosquito Plains I followed the ridge from Narracoorte southward to Mr. John Robertson's Station on the Mosquito Creek, which I take to be the northern boundary of what may be considered the Penola district. This ridge, which extends in an almost unbroken line to beyond Mount Gambier, forms the highest of the parallel terraces receding from the coast line to the eastern boundary of South Australia. A double chain of Hundreds, extending due north from MacDonnell Bay to Narracoorte, have been declared along its course, embracing an area of country 80 miles north and south by 20 miles east and west. The Mosquito Plains stretch from its western foot on the north to the next parallel range terminating in the Moy Hall and Killanoola country in the Hundred of Robertson, which includes the vast Bool Lagoon. Southward of the Killanoola head station and in the Hundred of Killanoola commences the rich agricultural country of which Penola is the practical centre. From the north-west corner of the Hundred, following a south-easterly course to Penola through Dr. Dixon's country and Mr. Riddoch's Woolshed paddocks, the soil is exceedingly rich and admirably adapted to agricultural operations. There are some swampy flats in [Killanoola, but they have been for the most part avoided in the surveys. Indeed one narrow strip of sections follows the course of a fine open bank, similar in form but richer in quality than the famous Moy Hall rises, with almost mathematical precision. Of course the freehold of such a bank has given a monopoly of the adjoining swampy ground in the past, but the drainage, amongst its other good results, will destroy all that kind of thing in the future.

The prevailing rule of this higher terrace appears to be that on the lower or westward slope of the ridge the soil consists of a black loamy deposit, and that on its higher levels first strong clays and then a light red earth and limestone obtain. It is singular that with such excellent agricultural resources at command Penola should have remained for so many years a purely pastoral district,

especially as vast quantities of flour, produced at Mount Gambier, were conveyed every year through the very heart of it to supply the towns and stations to the northward. As a matter of course, Penola might have easily intercepted the whole of this trade as the cost of cartage would necessarily have placed her Southern neighbors beyond the pale of competition. The new enterprise, which might as well have been developed years ago, is however fairly inaugurated now, and not only is farming becoming general around Penola but a steam flour mill is in operation there. Mr. John Riddoch, one of the members for the district and the owner of the large and valuable estates of Yallum Park and the Woolshed, has placed himself at the head of this onward movement. Last year he had 500 acres under crop, and this year he has 1,200. The average yield of last year was nearly 20 bushels to the acre, and there is little doubt that even larger results will be obtained. The whole breadth under crop has materially increased this year, and new ground is being cleared and broken up in every direction. Mr. Ralstone, and other land owners in the vicinity, have been stimulated to extend their agricultural operations; and Mr. R. McClure is going vigorously to work to demonstrate how tenant farming upon such land, and with such a climate, will repay industry and enterprise, A good deal of land has been let on lease for farming purposes, at 10s. per acre, with right of purchase at £5. I don't want to diverge into a political discussion just now; but let these facts be remembered when the opponents of land reform declare that the present system gives facilities to the farmer. The bulk of these very lands, which the settler who will improve and cultivate them cannot get on lower terms than I have named, and which keep his nose to the grindstone when he ought to be reaping a good reward for his labor, were alienated from the Crown at little more than £1 per acre as the result of the monopoly which the present system secures to capital.

There is very little to remark about the town of Penola itself. Approaching it from the north you are between fences all the way from Mosquito Creek, and in the winter time, by the confinement of the traffic to so narrow a limit, the stiff clayey soil, with the assistance of surface puddles, is pounded into a sort of hasty pudding in which the wheels of bullock drays sink to the naves, and mail coaches occasionally stick fast. Three miles north of the township, you get on to the "metal," and if you are not ungrateful bless Macadam. Presently you pass the new steam mill, indications of agricultural enterprise increase, and then a long line of scattered buildings attests Penola. There are a Police-station, cottage residences, a snug comfortable looking hotel, shops, more residences, stores, another hotel with a large open space and an air of the old fashioned coaching house about it, one pretentious structure—quite solitary in grandeur, and significant of shareholders—on either side of the main road, a few other shops and houses in lines at right angles thereto—and in a descriptive sense there is really nothing more to be said about Penola. The site and the surrounding country are too flat and thickly timbered, except where the axe has been wielded in favor of the plough, to enable a view of any consequence to be obtained, and lovers of the picturesque must look elsewhere to be gratified. But although in the past Penola has been little more than a break in a squatting solitude where mail coaches changed horses, stock agents made their head quarters, and stationmen drank beer, it will inevitably attain a position of usefulness and prosperity in the future. From the development of the agricultural resources which have until lately lain dormant at its door, it cannot fail to gather an accession of population, commercial importance, and material wealth. It occupies a fortunate position, not only as the actual centre of a district possessing an ample area of rich soil and a genial climate, but as being exactly midway between Narracoorte and Mount Gambier, far enough from them to be independent of both ; and as the necessary inland terminus of Victorian overland traffic on the one side, and of the drainage works and their connection with Rivoli Bay on the other. And it is a matter for congratulation that amongst the residents of Penola there are a number of enterprising and cultivated men whose efforts on behalf of certain useful public institutions have given the town—although it has been scarcely anything more than a station depot—an honorable prominence in the district. The Penola Institute, for instance, is quite a feature of the South-Eastern district, and its catalogue of works of reference, history, science, biography, law, philosophy, theology, poetry, and general and lighter literature, would well bear comparison with those of similar institutions in far larger centres of population. It is hoped that with the assistance of the Parliamentary grant, and the donations of neighboring residents, the building fund will soon suffice for the erection of a structure worthy of the really excellent library that has been accumulated, and of the position the Institute has assumed. In sporting matters too, and in the development of social gatherings associated therewith, which gave a welcome zest to the dull routine of life in a bush township, Penola has acquired an honorable distinction. Its race meetings, and race balls, its cricket matches, or kangaroo hunts, its Institute festivals, or simple convivial gatherings to honor a neighbor or visitor, are invariably characterised by a spirit of cordiality and good fellowship that produces, as it always must, the best results. Indeed, I may fairly say of Penola that the excellencies of its soil and climate in an agricultural sense are fully equalled by the social excellencies of its people.

Following the course of the terrace parallel with the province boundary, and southward towards Mount Gambier, you pass through a belt of inferior sandy country to Tarpeena, but by diverging slightly to the west you reach the lower slopes of the rise and the richer country about Kalangadeo.

It is a singular fact that the Dismal Swamp, which extends from Tarpeena over almost the whole of the Hundred of Mingbool, lies on a higher level than the surrounding country, or than the townships of both Penola and Mount Gambier. The surface water of the swamp is 213 feet above the sea level, and there is a fall to the Glenelg on the eastward as well as towards the sea on the west. Beyond the Dismal, still going to the southward, you emerge from this wide region of morass, the ceaseless cuckle of frogs, and the stunted timber of the dry banks surrounding sections of the swamp, upon the first indications of the far-famed Mount Gambier country. But now that we have arrived at last at the confines of the "garden" of South Australia, I must reserve for a new chapter the enumeration of its resources and whatever description I may be able to give of the unique glories of its scenery.

CHAPTER X.

The Mount Gambier District—Gambierton—The Lakes—Port MacDonnell: its Trade and Resources.

It is no exaggeration to say that Mount Gambier is one of the gems of Australia. Its scenery is unique and "sensational." I have travelled considerably, but nowhere else have I seen, nor even read of, such a view as may be obtained from any of the saddles of the Mount. Looking down upon the still, deep, almost black blue waters of the Lake, whose bed was once the crater of a volcano, the mind must be dead indeed that can resist the impulse to look back to the scene that must have been presented before flame, smoke, and lava yielded to the dominion of the element whose placid surface is barely

rippled now. Looking round upon the picture of fertility, the noble old forest gums, the luxuriant vegetation, the rich soil of decomposed volcanic ash, and the imprints of progress which industry and art have set upon the face of nature, it is difficult to match the prospect. I do not mean to imply that the other colonies cannot point to as good soil in exceptional localities, or to as perfect scenic beauty of a different type, or that our own Northern District does not far surpass the Mount in the extent of its agricultural resources, but I doubt if anywhere else in

Australia the same wealth of soil and climate, with beauty of scenery, can be obtained as within a radius of five miles from Mount Gambier.

But I am anticipating my story. Following the order of progress adopted in previous articles, I must ask my readers to remember that I left off at a point where the passage of the Dismal Swamp had been made, and continuing due south, indications of the better country of the Mount Gambier District began to prevail. Following that line we soon come again on to the metalled road which leads direct into Mount Gambier. You are now between fences, and signs of clearing and cultivation abound. The soil is light, and ferns—one of the chief pests of the district—are abundant, but, notwithstanding, agriculture seems to flourish. Every mile you advance the quality of the soil and the settled character of the country continue to improve. The land is gently undulating, and the road, straight and white, may be seen for miles a-head, surmounting each new rise, and, with scattered patches of green fences and gardens enclosing snug little cottages or farm homesteads, presenting a picture of rural beauty worthy of comparison with the noble highways of old England. Presently, when the summit of the last descent to the township is reached, a long string of cheerful-looking buildings nestling in a valley, and clusters of white houses peeping through the timber on the adjacent hill slopes, give the first view of Mount Gambier. Like the village of Grand Pré in the Arcadian land, "distant, secluded, and still," it lies "in the fruitful valley." Towering above it on the south, a stately sentinel of nature, is the Mount itself. Westward of the township the suburbs of Rosaville and Claraville are indicated by other groups of buildings, and the smoke from foundries and mill chimneys attests a centre of enterprise and industry.

The main thoroughfare of the township is the Commercial-road, which extends east and west for more than a mile to the suburbs already named. At the point where it is intersected by the main road from Penola to MacDonnell Bay, along the course I have followed, some of the best buildings in the town are situated. One corner is occupied by a large and commodious hotel erected by the late Mr. Mitchell, and now occupied by Mr. McKay. Opposite to it stands the National Bank; and a very handsome suite of banking premises have recently been added to the original building. Another corner is occupied by the Post-Office—a Government building which, unlike such erections in our more favored metropolis, is quite unworthy of the architectural style sustained by private house owners. The last corner has been recently purchased by the English, Scottish, and Australian Chartered Bank, upon which a new block of buildings will be erected. Turning eastward the principal buildings and places of business on either side of the road are the new Institute and Hall ; the *Mount Gambier Standard* and *Border Watch* Offices ; Long's South Australian Hotel ; a row of handsome shops, occupied by Mr. Aubrey ; Mr. G. M. Nobe's Furniture and Land Mart ; Mr. Williams's mill ; other shops, occupied by Brooks and Muirhead, A. Macgeorge, W. A. Crouch, N. A. Lord, &c. ; the present offices of the English and Scottish Bank, Mr. Finlay McKay's foundry, &c., &c. To the westward of the junction there are Blackwell Brothers' extensive premises, Mr. Clark's ironfoundry, Wehl & Co.'s mills, some handsome private residences, and a great variety of other buildings, devoted to innumerable purposes of trade and commerce, only to be found in a town that has acquired, as Mount Gambier undoubtedly has, the distinctive character of a local metropolis. Going southward from the junction of the roads I have named, there are the Telegraph Offices—a substantial two-storey building; Christchurch—one of the handsomest edifices of the kind in the colony; the Court-House, which is equally ugly and inconvenient; and the Police-Station. Higher on the rise of the Mount are Hedley Park, the elegant villa residence of Mrs. Mitchell, who, from the extent of her landed possessions in and around the township, may be considered "the lady of the manor" of Mount Gambier; the residence of Mr. E. H. Derrington; and finally, and most important of all, the Mount Gambier Hospital, one wing of which is now completed and in use. Of that more anon. It must not be supposed that I have in these few lines enumerated all the buildings in the town which are worthy of remark, but the list will suffice to give some idea of the extent and importance which—as a township—Gambierton has attained.

Before describing what may be specifically termed the Mount Gambier District, I wish to make one peculiarity of the position of the township clearly understood. So far as commercial importance, wealth, population, and resources are concerned, Gambierton is undoubtedly the metropolis of the South-East. But in a geographical sense it just as certainly fails to supply one of the most desirable conditions of a metropolitan town. If instead of being in an extreme corner of the South-East it were centrally situated its progress would have been even more marked than it is, and its local value far greater. But inasmuch as it lies on the direct highway to Port MacDonnell—which is bound to expand as the necessary outlet for the southern end of the district—as the country immediately surrounding it is almost fabulously fertile, and as it possesses sufficient advantages of scenery and climate, and facilities for sport, to attract numerous visitors from beyond its merely local limits, there is little danger that it will lose the pre-eminence it has attained. No doubt its development as the principal town of the district has resulted from the peculiar richness of the land around it, which has given profitable occupation to a large and industrious population, and the vested metropolitan interests it has acquired will not be easily disturbed; but there is nevertheless an anomaly in the capital of such a district being only 17 miles from the sea on the south, and about 20 miles from the province border on the east.

What may be considered the Mount Gambier District proper embraces the Hundreds of Blanche, Gambier, MacDonnell, and Caroline. North of Blanche and Gambier the Hundreds of Young and Mingbool will also be retained by the force of circumstances within the commercial relations of Port MacDonnell—essentially the port of Mount Gambier; and Kongorong, on the west, will probably be included within them also. Benara, from its contiguity to Lake Bonney and the drainage works, may be attracted rather to Rivoli Bay. These Hundreds, it will be found, comprise all the country of which I have not given already a close, and I think I may venture to say, accurate description. Their lines reach to the sea on the south, and to the province boundary on the east, and uniting on the north and west with the points to which my previous chapters have extended, will complete. "the South-Eastern District," as I undertook to describe it.

Immediately around the Mount, and within a radius of some four or five miles therefrom, the quality of the soil is of the richest character. On the surface it is a light friable compost of decomposed vegetable and disintegrated lava. The mould in its natural state is fine enough for garden beds, and its forcing properties are sufficiently apparent in the rapid vegetation which invariably follows a fall of rain. But it has one drawback, which applies more particularly to the soil on and adjoining the slopes of the Mount. There the subsoil is exceedingly porous, and however much rain may fall, it is so quickly absorbed that the crops, especially those which require moisture late in the summer, frequently suffer materially in consequence. Dr. Wehl, for instance, assured me that although the soil in his garden adjoining his private residence, on the Commercial-road, is of the finest description, he finds it almost impossible to raise any fine fruit there because of its excessive dryness. But there are veins of clay underlying the top soil in places, particularly in the Yahl paddocks, and on the fine farm best known as Mr. Andrew Beswick's, but recently purchased by Mr. Umpherston for something over £15 per acre; and there the productive capabilities might challenge comparison with almost any lands in the world. Mr. Beswick has taken heavier crops of wheat or wheaten hay off his paddocks year after year, burning the straw off the land and returning no manure at all, than any Essex farmer would even hope for on his best loams well manured, fallowed, and cropped on the four course shift, with clovers and turnips grazed on the land.

The famous Lakes constitute one of the chief lions of the Mount district. I have frequently had occasion to refer to them incidentally, and now I find it impossible to realise upon paper the grand type of supernatural beauty which the principal one of the three presents. It is called the Blue Lake, after the color which its placid waters always present. Its walls of lava rise almost perpendicularly to a height of some 200 feet above the water, and have a circumference on their summit of nearly four miles. The main road to Macdonnell Bay crosses the top of the ridge separating the Blue Lake from its lesser fellows, and from that point the best view of all three can be obtained. The middle Lake has but little water in a slight hollow, on a level with the larger basin, and many suppose it to result from drainage therefrom, but other authorities are equally positive that they have no connection. The Blue Lake was the main crater of the volcano, which, in former ages, belched out the ash and lava which now, in their decomposed state, constitute the peculiar richness of the soil around. The bed of the Valley Lake, which lies immediately beneath the highest peak of the Mount, was also a crater, but a smaller one. Attempts have been recently made to stock it with fish, and hopes are entertained of success. Local history only records one attempt to explore the Blue Lake by boat. It was made personally by Sir Richard Macdonnell, with a party of friends, and it is related that a cavernous passage was discovered, and that the party pushed their boat into its recesses until their lights were extinguished, and they were fain to return. In the very centre of Gambierton, at the junction of the main Adelaide-road, there is a large cave, in which the water rises to about the same level as in the Blue Lake, and it would be an interesting work to ascertain, if possible, whether it has, as it possibly may, any direct connection with the subterranean passage there.

About five miles from the Mount in almost any direction you get beyond the region of purely volcanic soil, and come again to the light red loam and limestone formation on the rises, and to the ordinary swamp soil or cold wet clays on the lower levels. Taking, for instance, the line of country from the Mount to the Glenelg river : this is all in the Hundred of Caroline, and the road passes through the new Government township of Caveton. Undulating ridges prevail, and the red soil and limestone. At places, particularly round the new township, the country is very cavernous, and the curious in such matters may find numerous specimens of fossil shells in excellent preservation. A good deal of settlement has taken place hereabouts, and I believe the farmers would do well enough but for sundry evils they have to contend with. A year ago a fire on the Mount Schanck run burnt them out, destroyed their crops and fences, and in some instances their homesteads. The kangaroo nuisance must be almost as fatal to them. I have already mentioned how the marsupials swarm in some parts of the district; but from Caveton to Glenelg it is wonderful that anything else can live at all. The country, except where the farmers have tackled the work of clearing and cultivation, is lightly timbered, chiefly with honeysuckle and sheoak, and covered with ferns, and every fern-bush seems to give cover to a brush kangaroo. You may pull up as you drive along the road, and from almost any point detect a score or two of little black noses, peaked ears, and bright eyes, the latter watching you in the most coolly critical way from behind as many ferns. If you are tempted to take your gun and walk a few yards off the road for a shot, scores more

of the little animals that you have not seen before will jump up all round you and make tracks in a series of merry bounds until the place seems alive with them. Besides these, you come every now and then on a mob of veritable foresters, with some booming old men, who will sit up quietly and stare you out of countenance, if you have no dogs to engage their attention otherwise. Of course, such an abundance of these pests is most injurious to the farmers, and until something is done to thin them down, or drive them back to the unsettled country, raising crops there will be a hazardous occupation, or it must involve almost ceaseless precautions.

The old boundary line of the colony was about two miles from the Glenelg, but now it will be shifted to the other side of the river, I believe. There may be some advantage to South Australia in including the sea-mouth of the Glenelg within her territory, and some people have been sanguine enough to advocate the formation of a port there. A work of the kind would, however, involve a heavy expenditure, for a sand-bank forms a barrier to the entrance, as in almost all Australian rivers. If that difficulty could be overcome and a channel kept open, a magnificent harbor could be obtained inside, and as the distance from Mount Gambier is only 22 miles, it might supersede Port MacDonnell as the port of the district. If the new boundaries are to be finally adjusted so as really to place the mouth within our territory, an examination of the place should at least be made before any further expenditure is incurred at MacDonnell Bay. At present very few travellers cross the Glenelg. There is a punt available for crossing carriages and stock, and as it is on the main line to Portland, it is occasionally, but very rarely, patronised. The locality is more frequently visited by shooting or picnic parties, to whose purposes it is especially adapted. There is a good house of accommodation on the Victorian side, and boats may be obtained for an excursion up the river, or down to its mouth. A more pleasant and enjoyable spot for a day or two's quiet rustication could hardly be desired, and sportsmen would find quite enough to do either with the gun, rod, nets, or dogs.

From Mount Gambier to MacDonnell Bay the country is more open, and having been longer settled and extensively cultivated, presents quite a different appearance. But in its first aspect it must have been very similar to the parallel line I have been describing, with the exception of the other extinct volcano called Mount Schanck, which is on the left of the road to the Bay, about ten miles from Gambierton. Settlement is extending in that locality wherever enterprising farmers have been able to invade the pastoral strongholds that have monopolised the country so long. Almost to the confines of the swamp which lies immediately behind the township of Port MacDonnell, and which ought to be drained at once, there are farms all the way from Mount Gambier, except where the iron heel of the Mount Schanck estate has stamped out the better purpose. From the Port the country extends north-westward through the Hundreds of Kongorong and Benara to the German Swamp District, which I have described in what I have written about the drainage scheme, and eastward through the Hundred of Caroline to the Glenelg.

Respecting Port MacDonnell itself, a few words of description are necessary. The bay—so-called—is formed by a slight curve of the coast line from Cape North-umberland on the west to Flint Point on the east, the distance between the two headlands being about five miles, and the greatest indentation three-quarters of a mile. Being fully exposed to the south, vessels are frequently compelled in heavy weather to leave their moorings and run out to sea, and it occasionally happens that even coasting steamers are unable to land either passengers or cargo. Moorings are laid down about a mile from the beach, and a jetty 976 feet long and going into five feet of water at low tide, was erected in 1862, but is already decayed. It is built with a fall, so that the height of the jetty above a boat alongside it is very slight. That, with the exception of a new lifeboat shed—which with the fatality of officialdom was built some feet too short for the boat it was intended for —is all that has been done to afford shipping facilities at a port which, although naturally inferior, can point to export and import returns second to very few in the colony. The Port was not established until 1860, the jetty was built in 1862, and in 1866 the declared value of its exports to other colonies had risen to £126,000, consisting mainly of wheat and wool; and nearly £7,000 was received in import duties. Besides the steady increase since 1866 to those figures must be added the exports to Port Adelaide or other ports within the colony, and the goods imported from Port Adelaide on which duty was paid there. It is assumed that the imports from Melbourne or other colonies represent only one-third of the import trade of the Port, and since the heavy duties have been levied in Melbourne, the proportion in favor of Adelaide, as already noted at Guichen Bay, has been materially increasing.

Prior to the declaration of MacDonnell Bay as a port of export, the trade of Mount Gambier and the adjacent district was divided between Guichen Bay and Portland. Now, of course, it is centred upon MacDonnell Bay, and it will so remain in spite of all adverse influences, unless, indeed, a more secure harbor can be afforded within about the same distance from Mount Gambier. I have mentioned the possibility of the mouth of the Glenelg as an alternative, but I have very little faith in the probability of its adoption, and Green Point, which was at one time strongly advocated, seems to have been abandoned even by its warmest friends. Assuming, then, that Mac-Donnell Bay will be the southern port of the district, it is obvious that some considerable expenditure will have to be incurred in supplying greater facilities for the shipping trade it will command. As to that, I shall have something more to say presently, when discussing the requirements of the district.

The Government buildings in the district consist of a Court-House, Customs-House, and Post-Offices, in a block ; and private enterprise has contributed two hotels and three spacious stores. The distance from the port to Mount Gambier is 17½ miles, and a good macadamised road has been constructed the whole distance. The cartage rates which have prevailed are £1 per ton, or 4d. per bushel for wheat. At the Port the charges for wheat have been 2½d. to 2½d. per bushel for agency, wharfage, &c., and 6d. per bushel freight by steamer to Melbourne, or 4d. by small sailing vessels. For wool, the Port charges have been 3s. per bale, and freight to Adelaide or Melbourne 7s. per bale dumped, or 8s. 6d. undumped. Insurance rates have been about equal to those prevailing at other ports, viz., 12s. 6d. per cent. against total loss by steamer, or 15s. to 20s. by sailing vessel, and 50 per cent. additional if free of particular average. It is probable, however, that the charges for wharfage, lighterage, &c., will be somewhat modified ; and certainly when better facilities are afforded they will be.

Cape Northumberland, ever to be remembered as the scene of the wreck of the ill-fated Admella, is about two miles from the port, and the lighthouse erected there merits some notice. It stands upon a rocky promontory about 40 feet above the sea level, and the surf which breaks at the foot of it seems to threaten to undermine the very foundations of the building. The lights used are alternately three green in a bunch, then three red, and then three white, the whole revolving with the utmost regularity. The motive power is derived from clockwork, which has to be wound up every two hours. The house is well fitted with all necessary instruments. Everything about the place is kept as bright as burnished gold, and on a clear night the light will show 30 to 40 miles out to sea. Three men, with their families, are located there, but the accommodation provided for them is quite inadequate.

Returning now to Mount Gambier, a few observations by the way will be interesting as to Dr. Browne's fine estate of Moorak. It lies to the south of Mount Gambier from one to four miles, and comprises 25,000 acres, bounded by the Punt or Glenelg River-road on the east, and by Mr. Cameron's Benara station on the west. The home station is situated on one of the lower slopes of the Mount, and the paddocks around it, some of which have been laid down in artificial grasses, present the very ideal of fertility. Farming operations are carried on on a large scale, independently of what is being done by the numerous tenantry to whom Dr. Browne has leased farms with a right of purchase. For years past 1,200 acres have been cropped with wheat. The year before last, as an experiment, the seed was sown after the soil had been merely har-, rowed, and was then trodden in. It was thought from the extreme looseness and friability of the soil that the plan would answer, but it did not. Now the ploughing, sowing and harrowing is done by contract for 15s. per acre, and as high an average all round as 20 bushels per acre has been obtained. Dr. Browne has already acquired something more that a merely local fame for the sheep he has introduced. He crosses Merinos with nearly pure Lincolns, and the result both for wool and carcase is found to be very satisfactory. During his late visit to England he selected ten pure Lincoln rams, nine of which were landed safely. They are remarkably fine animals, and will enhance the value even of the Moorak flocks. One of them shore 25 lbs. of wool. The estate is managed for Dr. Browne by Mr. Williams, and its natural advantages, and the various improvements which have been effected, will well repay inspection.

Mount Gambier possesses another scientific and enterprising agriculturist in Dr. Wehl, of the Claraville Mills. He has a considerable landed property in the district and farms largely himself. During the last year or two he has been demonstrating the value of flax culture and its adaptability to the district, and he has also been practising a series of experiments with artificial grasses which are especially interesting. His first trial was with cocksfoot and the Yorkshire fog, and the result was that the cocksfoot gave the most feed, and stood the heat and drought best, but the fog was less affected by the frosts which are frequent about th Mount. On a 40-acre paddock a good bottom of white clover and rye grass has been obtained, but the prairie grass has failed because it requires a clay subsoil. At Mr. T. A. Wells's farm in the Yahl Paddock, where that desideratum is obtained, it grows magnificently, and has been proved the most valuable grass to cultivate, but it is just as certain that it will not stand on the light porous subsoils about the Mount. In another paddock, where Dr. Wehl laid down six acres with 36 lbs. of mixed grasses, chiefly perennial and Italian rye-grass, Timothy, and a little clover, the Italian soon died out, but the perennial has stood well, and yielded a fine crop of hay the first year! Of about 40 other varieties of grasses experimented with, Dr. Wehl recommends the sweet vernal as calculated to stand dry weather well, and a feeding herb called Timpenalla, which is grown extensively in Germany, and has the reputation of being superior to clover. But the general result of his experiments is in favor of the prairie grass where there is a clay subsoil, and of cocksfoot where the subsoil is more porous. Messrs. Carl Wehl and Co. have a tannery in conjunction with the mills, and it is also worth noting that they have introduced the curing and tanning of kangaroo skins. They give as much as 7s. a dozen all round for the skins, and some of the squatters round about get a sufficient return under that head to pay the greater proportion of the expense of hunting down the marsupials. The other more prominent industries in Mount Gambier are the foundries of Mr. Chas. Clark and Mr. Finlay McKay, the furniture factory of Mr. Bristowe, and the breweries of Messrs. Gebhardt and Anderson. Both Mr. Clark and Mr. McKay have coach and implement factories attached to their establishments, and at Mr. Clark's any kind of castings can be done.

CHAPTER XI.

The Public Institutions of Gambierton.—On the Summit of the Mount.

It only remains now to notice some of the more important public institutions of Mount Gambier, before grappling with the material question of the requirements of the District as a whole.

The local Institute is, I think, fairly entitled to precedence, both from the spirit and liberality with which it is supported, and the practical advantages it affords. The Committees who have held office have for some years past worked very energetically on its behalf, and with much well-merited success. A fine building, which besides being architecturally ornamental, supplies ample accommodation for every necessary purpose of such a structure, has been lately erected, chiefly at the cost of the local residents. It has a spacious reading room, library, offices, and a magnificent hall. The library, although scarcely equal to that at Penola, is tolerably comprehensive, and is being constantly augmented. A museum has been commenced, and already a considerable collection of interesting objects has been obtained. And, also in connection with the Institute, it is the custom at suitable seasons of the year to give periodical literary and musical entertainments, which are generally well patronised, and afford a constant source of intellectual enjoyment. They are usually held once a fortnight ; the charge for admission is only sixpence, and the proceeds, which average something

like £100 per annum, are of course devoted to the purposes of the Institute. In other provincial towns more numerously populated than is Mount Gambier, the same practice might be adopted with signal advantage.

An Aborigines' Home has been established in the vicinity of the town, and is sustained mainly at the cost of Miss Burdett Coutts. Mrs. Smith is the Matron in charge, and she appears to be very zealous in the work of caring for and civilising any aboriginal children who will accept her protection. When I visited the Home it had twelve inmates, and four girls who had been resident there had been fitted for and placed in domestic service. Of these sixteen ten were half-castes. One little fellow, who spoke English fluently, announced himself as " Willie, Duke of Normandy ;" and another was introduced by the Matron as " Johnny Short," being named after the Bishop of Adelaide, who takes great interest in the institution, and administers Miss Coutts's charity on its behalf. All the inmates are descendants of the Penganka and Boandik tribes, who formerly occupied the country from Mount Gambier to Tatiara. The dominion of the Boandiks comprised the southerly portion of that area, and the Pengankas roamed from Penola northwards. They have but few full-bred representatives now, but the commingling of the white and black races is frequently evidenced, as amongst the inmates of the Home. Most of those who have had the advantages of Mrs. Smith's tuition and care have proved apt at learning, and but few of them have returned to their native state. They have been very subject to fevers and whooping cough, and the Matron spoke in the warmest terms of the kindness and constant attention manifested towards them by Dr. Peel, then the Assistant Colonial Surgeon resident at the Mount, who also supplied any necessary medicines at his own cost. It is to be regretted, however, that the accommodation at Mrs. Smith's disposal is but limited, and I think no one would object to the appearance on the next Estimates of the small sum that would be sufficient for the erection of a suitable building. Will the present Treasurer—who, as member for the district, ought not to overlook such a matter—take the hint?

The Farmers' Club is another institution peculiar to Mount Gambier, which has done considerable good and merits commendation. By peculiar to Mount Gambier, I don't mean that Farmers' Clubs are not common enough, but that in some of the objects it has had in view, it has set an example of its own. Besides the ordinary purposes of such Clubs it undertook the shipment and sale, through its agents, of the produce raised by its members, by means of which, in the first two years of the experiment, a reduction of 2½d. per bushel was effected on freight and shipping charges on wheat. Subsequently a still further reduction was obtained, and other advantages—in the supply of the latest market intelligence for the exclusive use of members, assistance in obtaining advances on produce, the importation of seeds, cornsacks, &c.—have been afforded. Much of the success attained in these matters is

admitted to be due to the business tact and perseverance of Mr. E. E. Maisey, who in the earlier years of the Club's existence acted as its Secretary. One of its latest undertakings, in the interest of its members, has been the appointment of a "Commission" of practical farmers to examine and report upon the quality and capabilities of the land affected by the drainage works. I am glad to find that the report of the deputation fully sustains the sanguine opinions I have expressed of what the agricultural value of the reclaimed flats will be when the works are completed, as they must be.

I should not be justified in omitting to notice the local press, as another public institution of which Mount Gambier may be justly proud. Few townships of equal population could support two such newspapers as those published there, and yet they both present undoubted evidences of prosperity. The *Border Watch* is very much the elder of the two, and it has acquired far more than a local reputation, particularly for its persistent advocacy of a liberal land reform, and the adjustment of the local land sales to the bona fide requirements of the agricultural settlers. Its proprietors have recently erected new and commodious offices in one of the best positions in the town. The *Mount Gambier Standard*, which was established four years ago, entered the lists as the especial advocate of the farming interest, and must have proved a formidable rival to its older brother. It is now owned and conducted by a gentleman who had the credit of promoting its first appearance, and who, although for some time past, until recently, devoted to other pursuits, made his mark in the literary profession when working actively in its ranks some years ago. Both papers are published bi-weekly, and their general character is highly creditable to their conductors.

There are some other institutions which come into the governmental category, which should be mentioned ; for instance, the Hospital and the Gaol. The Hospital is designed for the reception of invalids from all parts of the district, which, I suppose, will, in practice, be defined as from such localities as are nearer to the Mount than to Adelaide. With this view, the design of the building has been based upon a large scale, and some years will necessarily elapse before it is completed in its entirety. At present only one wing and a portion of the offices and outbuildings have been finished, but these present a striking if not very elegant appearance. The architecture is said to be of the Italian-Gothic order, and I suppose it will be pronounced rank heresy to describe even the section of the building that is erected as anything but beautiful in its outward form. But I must dare the imputation. I have looked long at the portion of the design which is completed, and I have a photograph of it before me as I write, but I cannot persuade myself that it is anything but unsightly. That it will be a structure magnificent in the extent of its masonry and commodiousness is indisputable ; but in my judgment a considerable proportion of the cost is thrown away upon elaboration and superfluities of architecture which haven't even beauty to commend them. For instance, there is to be a tower in the centre of each wing, and another in the centre of the main front. Neither of them, judging from the design, is worthy of the name, and the one that is erected is eminently suggestive of a compromise between the top of a pepper-castor and an extinguisher. Three such abortions would make hideous a finer pile of masonry than even this hospital will present. However, there is good accommodation inside, and

the site of the building is unexceptionable. For the latter circumstance Dr. Peel deserves all the credit. Just at the time that he first went to the Mount as Resident Medical Officer, the authorities had chosen a site for the Hospital near the Gaol, on the lower slope of the Mount, and within the influences of the heavy fogs which prevail at night in the valley at its foot, in which the town stands. Dr. Peel recognised at once the advantages of having the Hospital on a higher level, and urged his opinion so strongly at head-quarters that it was adopted and his choice of position accepted. This is just below the summit of the saddle which encloses the Valley Lake on the north, and quite above the highest point to which the fogs ever rise. The building, when completed, will have capacity for 72 beds, and the portion now in use will accommodate 32 patients; besides a cutaneous ward containing four beds. The centre front will be appropriated to the resident officer's apartments, and public reception rooms, &c., and each wing will have its separaed day room, bathrooms, earth closets, and padded rooms for hysteria cases. The outer walls are built with a three-inch flue throughout to afford ventilation and protection from damp. Two kinds of stone have been employed in the work. The one, the red dolamite so common to the district, which has almost the appearance of red granite, and the other a soft white coralline limestone. The latter has been used for the corners and dressings, and the contrast it presents to the red, or rather pink stone, is very striking. One advantage of the coralline limestone is that although in working it it can be easily cut by a common saw, it hardens by exposure to the atmosphere.

The Gaol, which stands much lower on the same slope as the Hospital, is a plain-looking building enough, and was evidently designed before the fashion was adopted of making the public pay through the nose for architectural filagree in Government buildings. It comprises two sections, each having a spacious yard, 160 feet by 100, with five cells attached to the one, and six to the other. These were intended for male and female departments, but the sex usually privileged has in this instance been made to give way to debtors under arrest. The whole place is badly arranged, and very insecure. Some time ago, at Guichen Bay, a prisoner escaped by boring a hole through the wall ; and the walls of all the cells were immediately lined with iron plates. I suppose the same precautions will not be taken at Mount Gambier Gaol until a prisoner has escaped from it by a similar expedient. The cells, too, are very badly ventilated, and there is no proper accommodation for sick prisoners, nor any means of enabling those who may be sentenced to hard labor to perform it. These circumstances all tend to support the opinion I have already expressed, that the maintenance of two Gaols in the district should be abandoned, and then by the concentration of the present expenditure sufficient accommodation and reasonable security might be afforded. And, as I have also pointed out, a new Police Station is very urgently required at Robe, and the building now used as the Gaol there would answer that purpose admirably.

I think I have enumerated now most of the important public institutions of Gambierton. Of course, there are the churches and chapels, but I don't want to involve myself in sectarianism by contrasting their belongings. Let me rather as the *finale* to the task of description I undertook,

invite those who may read these lines to imagine themselves making the ascent of Mount Gambier itself, to look down from its summit upon the wide-spread view of lakes, valley, town, plain, wood, hills, and ocean. There are two paths by which the top may be reached, one by Moorak, around the northern side of the Valley Lake, and the other by a more gradual ascent on its northern side from the wall, as it may be called, which separates the Middle Lake from the Great Blue Lake. The following levels will indicate something of this ascent. At the junction of the Commercial-road in Gambierton with the main Adelaide-road the height above the sea level is 124 feet. Following thence the main road to Port MacDonnell in one mile you gain the highest level of the road cut along the dividing wall between the two lakes, which is 263 feet above the sea, and 200 feet above the water in the Blue Lake. Turning now to the right, in something less than another mile, you will reach the very pinnacle of the Mount, on which the Trig station is placed, but in that distance you must climb nearly 400 feet higher, the Trig being 625 feet above the sea level. But the view will repay all the pains required to obtain it. There are the lakes enclosed by almost perpendicular walls of lava, evidently deposited in distinct layers by the eruptions of successive ages ; and a smaller crater, quite dry, known as the Devil's Punch Bowl. The Moorak homestead lies below you on one slope, the Hospital on another, and the township and the suburbs of Rosaville and Claraville in the valley at their foot. Further northward you may trace the main road to Penola, marking by its white line the undulations it crosses, and continually varied by the snug homesteads that stud its course. To the north-west open fields and other homesteads, and beyond them the Glencoe country and the Mount Burr Range; to the west Mount Muirhead, the flats, the ridge which has been pierced by the drainage "Gaps," and then the white line of sandhills skirting the beach, and beyond it the Southern Ocean. Following its line to the southward you may discern Cape Northumberland, the lighthouse, and Port MacDonnell, with its cluster of white buildings; and on the eastward the picture is closed in by the range of hills lying beyond the Glenelg. In a direct line with Port MacDonnell Mount Schanck rears its rugged peak in solitary grandeur like a pyramid on a plain, and nearer still the mysterious windings of the main road are plainly seen, and suggest a doubt of the sanity of the surveyor who selected for its course two sides of a triangle where one might have been adopted with so much evident

advantage. Eye or mind can scarcely tire in contemplation of the scene, and I am the more earnest in advising all persons who have the opportunity, to see it for themselves, because I am fully convinced that any description within my power to give would fail to realise its varied beauties and many features of material interest.

And now, having traversed the district in every direction, and recorded its natural features and its dormant and developed resources as accurately as my powers of observation have enabled me, I must claim the privilege of concluding my descriptive labors upon literally the highest point in the district. The pilgrimage thereto has been a pleasant one to me, and I trust the story of the information I gained by the way has not been altogether unprofitable to those who have been at the trouble of perusing it.

CHAPTER XII.

THE REQUIREMENTS OF THE DISTRICT.

The descriptive chapters which I have now brought to a conclusion would be manifestly incomplete if not supplemented by some allusion to the public requirements of the district. In my introductory notice, written it must be admitted nearly two years ago, I proposed to describe first the natural resources of

the district, and the progress of their development; and then to explain what —after a careful study of the whole question—might appear to be its just claims upon the fostering care of a paternal Government. I have kept this purpose in view in all that I have written, and I cannot but feel strengthened in the views I have expressed by the fact that although my descriptive work has been extended over so long a period, no reason has been shown, nor have any circumstances transpired, to suggest the withdrawal or qualification of any remark embodied in the foregoing pages. I approach therefore this other material question of the requirements of the district in full confidence that I have correct and complete data from which to deduce conclusions.

I may safely commence with the assertion, that hitherto the district has received nothing like its fair proportion of public expenditure. A return laid on the table of the House of Assembly in the session of 1868-9 proved the amount received by the Government up to Dec. 31, 1868, from the sales of Crown lands within the Counties of Grey and Robe to have been £703,796, and the total expenditure upon roads, bridges, and jetties has been something like £100,000. These figures alone would prove a just claim against the Government, but there are many other reasons to be given on behalf of the district. It will well repay a liberal expenditure, if wisely ordered, upon the extension of facilities for traffic and shipment; and it is also worth the while of South Australia to attempt to inspire in the minds of the South-Eastern people greater confidence in national justice than the course of past legislation has occasioned. In the session of 1867 there appeared to be a Parliamentary desire to spend money freely enough in the district, without much regard to actual requirements. A Bill was passed authorising a loan of something like £300,000 for the construction of a railway from Narracoorte to Gambierton, and, notwithstanding the manifest absurdity of making a town 17 miles inland the terminus of such a line, people were satisfied

to attribute it rather to inconsideration than to injustice. Another line from Narracoorte to Lacepede Bay was also promised, and with these somewhat magnificent prospects as to expenditure, no one grumbled at the curtailment of the usual vote for road construction. But last session the railway scheme was shelved altogether, and the district, after being in this way simply cheated out of a year's expenditure upon its roads, is very little better off as to its facilities for traffic than it was before the apparent but delusive willingness to concede justice to the South-East was proclaimed. This has unquestionably excited, and very justly so, strong feelings of dissatisfaction and distrust, which will only be removed by a prompt and practical manifestation on the part of the Legislature of a determination to atone adequately for its injustice and neglect.

Necessarily the most urgent requirement is the extension, as far as practicable, of facilities for the conveyance and shipment of produce. At present, with the exception of road construction in the Mount Gambier end of the district, and some jetty expenditure at Port MacDonnell and Robe, scarcely anything has been done to promote that purpose. Large areas of land have been sold at much less than the value they might have commanded if even an assurance of the the construction of roads or railways had been given; and as another result, pastoral monopoly has been sustained where agricultural settlements should have been flourishing long ere now. When will our legislators be convinced that palatial public buildings in the City of Adelaide are of far less importance to the general interests of the community than works which would promote the settlement of the country and the development of its resources? Such phrases may be axiomatic and hackneyed, but they cannot be too often dinned into the ears of the Parliamentary blunderheads, who sacrifice national interests to the greed of the metropolitan building trade. This by the way. In considering how this first requirement of the South-East can be best supplied, we have to deal at the outset with the difficulty of sustaining and maintaining communication with four ports on a seaboard of less than 150 miles. It has always been a question with me whether a multiplicity of shipping places—and the consequent scattering amongst them of expenditure, which, if concentrated, would be so much more effective—is really beneficial. It would be useless, however, to argue the proposition here. There are already three established ports on the coast-line of the South-East, and a fourth—Rivoli Bay—although once abandoned, will be necessarily revived with the settlement of the drained lands in its vicinity. To have to discuss the relative capacities for usefulness, and claims to preference, of all these places is not an alluring task, because one cannot be impartial in such a matter without exciting some local jealousies. But I hope I shall be able to show reasons enough to disarm mere prejudice as to the conclusions I shall submit.

Of course the partisans of each port make its particular features the Alpha and Omega of their argument. I shall venture, on the contrary, to take the country to be accommodated as my starting point. For instance, the Tatiara district contains a large extent of good country fit for agricultural settlement. The good people of Kingston would, of course, demand that that place should be adopted as the port of export for Tatiara, and the partisans of Robe would be equally positive in asserting superior claims to Kingston. But let us see how

Tatiara would be affected. From Border Town to Kingston is something less than 65 miles; and to Robe a trifle over 80 miles. The character of the intervening country is pretty nearly alike on both lines, while, in point of distance, Tatiara produce would have a clear advantage of more than 15 miles in going to Kingston. Then comes the question of the relative merits of the ports. If the nearest port were very much the worst, it might be preferable to go the longer distance for the greater safety and convenience. But the answer is very easily given from the published opinions of the best authorities. Kingston, or Port Caroline, is certainly the best natural harbor on the seaboard of the South-East, and a comparatively small expenditure upon a jetty and approaches would render it incomparable as a place of shipment. Guichen Bay unquestionably ranks next, and but for the blunder—for which its author should be made to smart—of turning the new jetty into shallow water, reasonable facilities would have been already supplied there. The north end of Rivoli Bay may with some considerable expenditure be rendered a convenient shipping-place; and Port MacDonnell ranks last as to natural advantages. Therefore, whenever the Tatiara district is settled for agricultural purposes, it will necessarily find an outlet for its produce at Lacepede Bay. I have stated this instance now merely to illustrate the process of reasoning by which I am guided in expressing an opinion as to the means that should be adopted to facilitate the export of the produce of the district.

For precisely the same reasons which will inevitably connect Tatiara with Kingston, the latter place will command the trade of all the northern end of the district between, say, Salt Creek on the north and the parallel of Mount Benson on the south, besides considerable gleanings from beyond the Victorian border. This will comprise the Narracoorte, Morambra, Padthaway, Binnum, and Tatiara country ; in fact, the entire northern area of the district. No doubt, as long as Mr. Ormerod's business connections are retained at Guichen Bay the perfect adjustment these natural laws and their consequences will be delayed, but in view of the certain development of Lacepede Bay on the one side, and of Rivoli Bay and Port MacDonnell on the other, it appears an unavoidable conclusion that the port of Robe cannot command permanently anything more than a purely local trade. Its limits, I think, will be Mount Benson on the north, and Lake St. Clair on the south, extending inland as far as Killanoola. Rivoli Bay will be the nearest and most convenient outlet for the reclaimed lands in the County of Grey, extending from Lake St. Clair on the north to the German Swamp on the south ; while, if the proposal to lay down a light line of rails on the embankment of the main drain to Penola is carried out, even the trade of that locality may be to some extent attracted there. MacDonnell Bay will necessarily retain the trade of all the southern end of the district as far north, at all events, as Penola, and possibly to Mosquito Creek. I am certain that these outlines indicate the limits of the country which must in the natural order of things become attached to each of these ports. So long as the pastoral lessees retain possession of the country in the north of the district many of them who now ship their wool through Ormerod & Co. at Robe will no doubt continue to do so, but it would be a fatal error in legislation if only the present settlement, and not

the future occupation, of the country were to be considered. Roads or railways are not asked for for the squatters, but to promote the "opening up" of the country, and its settlement for a better purpose than the maintenance of a sheep upon two square miles of it. Presently, when Narracoorte and Border Town will be the centres of agricultural industry, the value of the land, and the profitable employment of that industry, will depend in a great measure upon the facilities given for the export of produce. It would be therefore a grievous error to ignore the nearest and best place of shipment by constructing a main artery of communication to any other port. I think it will be admitted that that simple and very obvious proposition disposes at once of the claims which have been set up on behalf of Port MacDonnell and Robe in opposition to Lacepede Bay for the trade of Narracoorte and Tatiara. I have shown already how the question would stand as to the Tatiara traffic, and now with regard to that of Narracoorte. It is just 81½ miles from Narracoorte to Port MacDonnell, and 51 miles to Lacepede Bay, with a bad port at the end of the long distance, and a good one at the end of the shorter line. What arguments can be more conclusive ? In face of them it appears marvellous that even a South Australian Parliament should have passed an Act to authorise the construction of a railway from Narracoorte to Mount Gambier (64 miles), when a good port could have been reached in 13 miles less than a town 17½ miles inland. The argument always used against the Lacepede Bay line is, that the country between Kingston and Narracoorte is bad, and between Narracoorte and Mount Gambier it is good. Granted, in general terms. But there are large areas of good country around Narracoorte, at Morambra,

Tatiara, and Lake Cadnite, all of which are nearer to Lacepede Bay than to any other port, and it is the future agricultural settlement of those localities which must be considered. Would any farmer elect to send his produce 80 miles for shipment, if he could reach a better port in 30 miles less?

Now, then, I will admit that there is an urgent necessity for the immediate accommodation of the agricultural settlement which has actually taken place in the Mount Gambier district, and is extending to Penola. The necessity is even more pressing than for the connection of Narracoorte with the seaboard. The two things required are the best means of communication with the nearest port, and reasonable improvements there. From Penola southward the nearest port is MacDonnell Bay. The first question, then, is, should a railway or a road be constructed between those two places? Now let us look at the facts. From MacDonnell Bay to Mount Gambier, 17 miles and a-half, there is as good a macadamised road as in any part of the colony. From Mount Gambier to Penola is 32 miles, and the road has been macadamised for about half the distance, consequently only some 16 miles have to be made to complete a good stone road from Penola to MacDonnell Bay. It becomes a question, therefore, between 16 miles of Macadam at say £1,200 per mile, and 49½ miles of railway at some £3,000 per mile, more than 30 miles of which would run parallel with a stone road already made. The conclusion I am therefore forced to is, that the immediate completion of that stone road, with a branch to Kalangadoo, and even its extension northward towards Narracoorte, is a just and reasonable requirement of the district, but that the railway is unnecessary, and that its con-

struction, under the circumstances, could not be justified. Neither do I think the railway would be so beneficial as the road, even if the road had not been made, and it were merely a question which should be adopted. For this reason. From the very fact that the country is good—with the exception of the Tarpeena scrub—agricultural holdings already extend or will soon be formed along the entire line. The farmers find profitable employment for their teams on the road, when otherwise they would be idle, and this advantage would be altogether lost to them if a railway replaced the road. Indeed, I think it may be accepted generally that wherever a choice has to be made between a railway and a road—the construction of both being impossible—the road will be best for short distances through a farming district, and the railway will answer better to bridge as it were a long stretch of bad country separating two points of settlement which require connection. Of course the conformation of the country, and the materiel available for construction, will largely affect the issue, but I have very little doubt about the general correctness of the proposition, and I am quite certain that the large majority of the Mount Gambier farmers would prefer an expenditure of say £50,000 upon the completion of the stone road to Narracoorte, and £100,000 upon the improvement of Port MacDonnell—£150,000 in all—to the proposed outlay of nearly double the amount upon the construction of the railway from Narracoorte to Gambierton alone. The improvement of Port MacDonnell is, under any circumstances, a necessary and just requirement. Assuming that no better site for the port can be obtained—and I think that may be admitted—it ought to be rendered at least safe and convenient for the large trade it is certain to retain.

I cannot pretend to discuss the various propositions nautical men have made respecting it. Whether a breakwater, or a new jetty with an L or a T head, or any other scheme would be best I don't know, but it is very evident that to provide better facilities for shipping than exist now is an immediate duty which the public Treasury owes to the district. With that duty fulfilled, and a good stone road completed to Narracoorte, justice would be done to the settlers at about half the cost to the country at large that the ridiculous project of constructing a railway from one inland town to another would have involved.

These requirements being supplied to a portion of the district already thickly populated, next in importance will be the extension of facilities for traffic and, shipment that will encourage the settlement of those other localities now monopolised by sheep, but which are capable of sustaining a large farming population. These may be defined as, besides the drained flats, Narracoorte Morambra, parts of Padthaway, Tatiara, Lake Cadnite, and a considerable area of the Mosquito Plains south-west of Narracoorte. The necessities of settlement on the reclaimed flats will be mainly met by the establishment of a port at Rivoli Bay, and the construction of roads or light lines of rail on the embankments skirting the main drains. The other localities I have named will find their natural and best outlet at Lacepede Bay, and, in accordance with what I have expressed above, I am satisfied that the best means of communication that can be given will be by a light railway thence through Narracoorte to the Victorian border, with a branch, when necessary, by Morambra towards Tatiara, or to Lake Cadnite. It would bridge over the intervening bad country far more effectually than a road would; it

would certainly tempt some of the Victorian traffic across the border, and it would afford in every respect the best means of transit from the country I have indicated to the nearest and best port of shipment. It is also worthy of remark that such a line would be available for mail and passenger purposes on the main line from Adelaide to the Mount, which—in addition to its other disadvantages—a railway from Guichen Bay would not be. And, also, the drainage of the flats at the northern end of the district would be materially assisted by the construction of the line, which in crossing the flats would intercept the natural fall of the swamp waters to the north-west. The excavations necessary for the embankments of the line would leave large parallel drains, and culverts at the foot of each ridge on the western side of the flats would afford a ready means of escape to the waters they would receive.

When all the circumstances which bear upon this enterprise come to be fully and impartially considered the Legislature will, I think, be compelled to adopt it. I do not claim that its immediate execution is so urgent as the supply of the requirements of Mount Gambier and Penola, where settlement is so much advanced, but it may be fairly said that the sooner it is undertaken the sooner will South Australia experience the advantages her South-Eastern territory is capable of affording.

Of course some expenditure will be required at Lacepede Bay in connection with such a work, but fortunately Nature has been so lavish in her gifts there, as far as the harbor is concerned, that little more than an extension of the jetty and decent approaches to it will have to be given at the public cost.

I have now enumerated what I take to be the most important requirements of the district, and I have shown— as I promised to do—how it appears, by a careful consideration of all the facts affecting the question, they may be best supplied. My opinions may cost me some opposition, perhaps even enmity—for I know party feeling on the subject sometimes waxes warm—but I have written without regard to any other influences than those of reason and truth. And I may hope at all events that in recounting some other minor claims which the district may justly prefer to Parliament, I shall sail upon a smoother sea.

There is the question, for instance, of mail communication. Notwithstanding the great improvements which have been made in the service, the time might be even further lessened, and the journey rendered much easier to passengers than it is now. The navigation of the lakes has been most successfully incorporated in the route, and a comparatively small expenditure will enable the steamboat trip to be extended on the smooth waters of the Coorong to Salt Creek. The scheme has been reported upon over and over again. Its perfect feasibility and great usefulness are admitted by the best authorities; but yet nothing more is done. There would be, besides the gain of time and rest for passengers in the mail service, a material advantage to the settlers along the stream, and in the scrub about Salt Creek, if the work were done. It has been estimated that £5,000 would be more than sufficient for the purpose; and I must include the opening of the Coorong to the navigation of vessels of a light draught as one of the requirements of the district, which would be of great advantage not only to the settlers in its locality but to the public generally.

The completion of the drainage scheme I need hardly mention, because the necessity for that is self evident. I have, in preceding articles, given all the details of cost, incurred and estimated, and the fact must not be lost sight of that every day's delay in the completion of the work is so much time lost in the realization of the great advantages it will entail. No doubt the squatters whose runs will be cut up by the settlement of the reclaimed lands will use all their influence to shelve the work, and, with the present Treasurer in office, it is possible he may evince his gratitude for the support he received at the late election by discovering difficulties in completing it. But, notwithstanding all such opposition, the work *must* go on. If funds cannot be obtained from any other source, they may be fairly raised by loan; and for every pound expended there will be ten pounds of actual value, as the consequence of reclamation, to set against it. And although my assertion in an earlier chapter of this work that the Maria Creek Swamp is destined to become the Warrnambool of South Australia has excited some "sarcastical" rejoinders, my merry critics have not given a shred of evidence to impugn its truth. I repeat now that when Mr. Goyder's drainage scheme is completed, not only the Maria Creek Swamp, but large areas of the reclaimed lands lying near Rivoli Bay and Lake Bonney, will be admirably adapted for the growth of the potato and other root crops; and as in each case a port of shipment will be close at hand, I have no fear for my prediction, and the scoffers in the meantime shall be welcome to their satire.

Allusion has already been made in these columns to the difficulties which have been experienced in the district in consequence of the uncertainty of the tenure of pastoral lands. A large number of the leases expire in June, 1870 ; and in view of that fact, and the doubts about obtaining renewals, station improvements have been stopped to a great extent. Now, although I would most strenuously maintain that the squatter should in all cases give way to the farmer, I cannot think it to be wise that unnecessary restrictions should be imposed upon pastoral enterprise. Until the agricultural lands of the South-East are required for the better purposes of settlement, the lessees should be confirmed in their possession, of course at a valuation to be periodically renewed. The agricultural settlement of all the available land in the district will necessarily take some years to accomplish, and until then the pastoral occupiers should be encouraged rather than thwarted in their enterprise. It is unfortunate that the question of the renewal of leases expiring in 1870 has not been dealt with earlier, but Parliament will soon reassemble, and this ought to be one of the first matters to engage its attention. It is quite possible to encourage agricultural settlement without being impolitic and unjust to pastoral interests.

It is scarcely necessary to enumerate all the items of accommodation which are required in the various townships. I have alluded to the necessity for improved approaches to the Kingston jetty, for a new Court-House and Police-Station at Robe, and for better postal and telegraphic arrangements at Kincraig. The Local Court at Kingston has been established, to the great advantage of the settlers, and the Telegraph Office has been completed there, and the line opened. At Gambierton some improvements might be beneficially effected, which its metropolitan character requires. For instance,

a constant and copious water supply might be easily afforded, and I believe the enterprise might be made remunerative with good management. Several schemes have been proposed—one to lay down a main from Lake Leake or Lake Edward, and another to raise a supply to a sufficient height from the Blue Lake. I think the latter proposal would be the most economical. When the Hospital works were in progress Mr. McKenzie fixed a force pump in the Valley Lake, by means of which he raised an abundant supply of water for all purposes a height of 240 feet. The whole cost was only £30, and one man could raise 150 gallons per hour. Mr. John Barrow, a civil engineer well-known at Mount Gambier, has prepared plans for supplying all the requirements of the townsfolk from the Blue Lake, and the Government might fairly extend some encouragement to such an enterprise. Or why should not a Corporation be formed for Gambierton, and the work be made a municipal undertaking ? There are several other desirable improvements, which, if assisted by the Government, could be more appropriately effected and maintained by a Corporation. A flight of steps cut to the level of the Blue Lake would render its still broad waters available for boating purposes, and a circular carriage drive might be laid out on the summit of its banks, which could scarcely be excelled for natural beauty in the world. An admirable site for a botanic garden might be obtained on the lower inner slopes of the Valley Lake, and some expenditure upon even that object would have useful, as well as pleasant, results. In these and several other respects, by a trifling outlay, Mount Gambier might be invested with so many new charms as, combined with its rare natural advantages, would render it one of the most delightful places of abode in the Australias. And surely South Australia would not grudge some cost for the setting of one of her brightest gems.

I have one other suggestion to offer. Might not the colony afford its Governors a summer residence at Mount Gambier? A more suitable locality could not be named in the colony, or one that would afford a more material and welcome change of climate and pursuits. The temporary residence of a Governor there would also have the effect of inspiring a more thoroughly South Australian spirit in the people than prevails now. Instead of a sense of isolation from the seat of government, and of neglect by the Legislature, a bond of sympathy and mutual interest would be directly established, and the results would certainly be beneficial. If, indeed, the public generally understood the South-Eastern district better than they do—and I hope what I have written may be a means to the end—very little more would be heard of injustice and neglect. If a vice-regal sojourn at the Mount became an event of each recess, many of our "governing" notabilities would follow the fashion, and the resources of the district *would be*, as a consequence, better known and more justly appreciated than they are now. I hope that the realization of some such "improvement" as this is not far distant, and that even before the demand for a second edition of the work I am now concluding has arisen, the hands of good fellowship will have been mutually extended from Adelaide and Mount Gambier, and united in a hearty grip symbolical of an indissoluble alliance in spirit, as well as in the letter of intercolonial boundaries.

THE END.

INDEX TO MAP.

NOTE.—The numbers of the leases noted below correspond with the numbers on the map, and will indicate all particulars respecting the runs, of which the boundaries are also marked.

PASTORAL LEASES SITUATE IN THE SOUTH-EASTERN DISTRICT.

No. of Lease.	Name of Lessee.	Name of Station.	Area	Rent.	Assesmt.	Expiry of Lease.
				£ s. d.	£ s. d.	
60	T. & J. Dodd ...	Coorong ...	4	15 0 0		June 30, '70
65	J. & A. Cooke	Maria Creek ...	5	18 15 0		"
148	John Binnie ...	Wirrega ...	64	966 0 0		"
149	James Gordon	Cannawigra W.	70	812 12 0		"
150	Do.	Do. E.	37	412 12 0		"
151	T. H. McLeod	Nalang ...	53	863 0 0		"
152	Do.	Do. E.	68	1135 8 0		"
153	Patrick Kelly	Swede's Flat ...	23	105 8 0		"
154	Bryan Cussen	Bangham	31	56 0 0		"
155	A. McArthur ..	Marcullet	32	164 4 0		"
156	Robert Lawson	Padthaway N. ...	34	301 12 0		"
157	Do.	Do.	50	835 0 0		"
158	Walter Laidlaw	Lake Roy ...	17	126 16 0		"
159	Mary Oliver ...	Morambro ...	103	1428 16 0		"
a159	Alexr. Davidson	Messemurray, E. & W.	20	158 4 9		"
160	H. & D. O. Jones	Conkar ...	108	675 0 0		"
161	Do.	Cadnite ...	34	430 0 0		"
162	Do.	Binnum Binnum	31	15 10 0		"
163	James Affleck	Kybybolite ...	65	354 12 0		"
164	Alexr. Davidson	Messemurray ...	9	4 10 0		"
165	Thos. Magarey	Narracoorte ...	35	407 6 9		"
166	A. Smith	Hynam and Broadmeadows	16	205 2 0		"
168	Wm. Robertson	Woolgoburg, Moy Hall	17	130 11 4		"
171	Henry Seymour	Killanoola, W. ...	30	141 8 8		"
174	D. McArthur ...	W. of Hundred of Killanoola	17	85 0 0		"
175	Do.	Do.	4	16 0 0		"
186	John Ellis	German Flat ...	8	50 0 0		"
194	Geo. Glen ...	Mayura ...	84	468 0 0		"
195	Ann Cameron...	Near Rivoli Bay	13	47 8 0		"
a195	Thos. Pether ...	Coonunda ...	20	60 0 0		"
b195	John Ellis	Lake Bonney ...	6	23 0 0		"
196	T. D. Seymour	Mt. Benson ...	47	268 12 0		"
197	Stockdale & Ormerod	Woolmit ...	56	274 16 0		"
198	Andrew Dunn	Murrabinna ...	47	130 12 0		"
199	James Brown	Tilley's Swamp	50	138 0 0		"
200	Do.	Avenue Range ...	83	270 10 0		"
201	Stepn. Jeffrey	Callendale ...	36	18 0 0		"
202	Geo. Ormerod	Mt. Scab ...	36	93 16 0		"
203	John Hensley	Cairn Bank ...	80	40 0 0		"
211	A. Johnson ...	Mt. Muirhead ...	71	388 8 0		"
212	Ann Cameron	Wattle Range ...	25	38 16 0		"
213	Stephen Jeffrey	Sheaoak Range	31	144 8 0		"
214	A. Johnson ...	Rivoli Bay ...	15	64 8 0		"
215	Edwd. Stockdale	Lake Hawdon, W. ...	13	82 4 0		"
a215	Thos. Magarey	Do., E. ...	37	70 0 0		"

No. of Lease	Name of Lessee	Name of Station	Area	Rent £ s. d.	Assessmt. £ s. d.	Expiry of Lease
216	Alexr. Pearson	Reedy Creek	39	226 0 0		June 30, '70
217	J. W. & M. McInnes	Crower	88	193 8 0		"
218	Chas. Stewart	Avenue Flat	46	86 0 0		"
a218	Wm. Stewart	View Bank	42	88 0 0		"
b218	R. N. Falloon	St. Helena	26	70 12 0		"
219	Geo. Ormerod	Biscuit Flat	17	8 10 0		"
a219	A. Dunn	Conmurra	17	102 0 0		"
220	Do.	Conmerry	25	58 0 0		"
221	Thos. Morris	Bowaka	55	27 10 0		"
222	A. Dunn	Blackford	36	147 0 0		"
223	J. W. & M. McInnes	Baker's Range	40	150 10 0		"
224	P. Kelly	Monster, N. Block	27	138 0 0		"
225	Do.	Do. S. do.	10	44 0 0		"
226	John Baker	Parnka	7	15 0 0		"
a226	A. Scott	Witalara, Coorong	6	5 0 0		"
b226	P. Macdonald	Do.	5	14 0 0		"
c226	Geo. Young	Coolatoo	1	5 0 0		"
228	Thos. Taylor	Fairview	42	73 12 0		"
284	J. W. & M. McInnes	Crower	40	20 0 0	63 6 8	June 30, '67
292	Thos. Morris	Bowaka	26	13 0 0	41 3 4	Dec. 31, '67
310	Bryan Cussen	Bangham	17	8 10 0	21 5 0	"
320	A. Dunn	Conmerry	34	17 0 0	52 8 4	"
346	George Hayes	E. of Mount Benson	2	1 0 0	3 10 0	June 30, '68
354	Edwd. Crow	Mount Bruce	96	558 16 0		June 30, '70
355	Saml. P. Lord	Avenue south of Reedy Creek	75	142 8 0		"
a355	Tilley & Ormerod	Do. N. do.	50	258 14 0		"
356	Thos. McKellar	Konnetta	55	254 0 0		"
a356	Ormerod & Tilley	Gillap	79	345 8 0		"
357	Thos. Magarey	N. Woakwine	37	137 16 0		"
a357	Archd. Johnson	S. Do.	62	214 8 0		"
358	Step. Jeffrey	Lake St. Clair	11	5 10 0		"
a358	Geo. Bunn	Do.	3	12 12 0		"
b358	Geo. Ormerod	Do.	9	37 16 0		"
406	Step. Jeffrey	Callendale	33	16 10 0	66 0 0	June 30, '69
450	Do.	Do.	18	9 0 0	24 15 0	"
461	Alexr. Pearson	Reedy Creek	12	6 0 0	20 0 0	June 30, '70
479	Geo. Glen	Mayura	10	5 0 0	10 0 0	"
484	Henry Seymour	Killanoola, W.	25	12 10 0	45 16 8	"
493	James Foote	Tilley's Swamp	27	13 10 0	32 12 6	Dec. 31, '70
539	Mary Oliver	Morambro	20	10 0 0	40 0 0	"
574	Patrick Kelly	Monster, N. Block	10	5 0 0	9 3 4	Mar. 31, '71
578	Ewen Cameron	Wattle Range	17	8 10 0	17 0 0	Sept. 30, '71
599	Henry Jones	Conkar	10	5 0 0	10 16 8	Dec. 31, '71
663	J. B. Hack	E. of Salt Creek	20	10 0 0	11 13 4	June 30, '72
696	J. G. J. Ker	Near Tilley's Swamp	30	15 0 0	12 10 0	Dec. 31, '71
712	Henry Jones	Conkar	16	8 0 0	4 0 0	"
719	Mary Oliver	Do.	8	5 0 0	6 13 4	June 30, '73
720	Henry Jones	Do.	8	5 0 0	6 13 4	"
732	Harding & Bunn	Near Monster Mt.	12	6 0 0	6 0 0	Sept. 30, '73
778	James Foot	Tilley's Swamp	29	14 10 0	6 0 10	Dec. 31, '75
782	George Bunn	Two Wells	15	7 10 0	8 15 0	June 30, '74
787	J. & A. Cooke	E. of Coorong	22	11 0 0	14 13 4	June 30, '74
797	James Foot	Tatiara	18	9 0 0	10 10 0	"
807	J. & A. Cooke	E. of Coorong	23	11 10 0	13 8 4	Mar. 31, '74
809	S. & C. Herriot	Near Two Wells	22	11 0 0	12 16 8	"
810	James Hooper	Binnie's Look-Out	54	27 0 0	27 0 0	"
820	George Bunn	Two Wells	15	7 10 0	10 0 0	June 30, '74
822	R. B. Smith	N.E. of Salt Creek	15	7 10 0	7 10 0	"

No. of Lease.	Name of Lessee.	Name of Station.	Area.	Rent. £ s. d.	Assessmt.	Expiry of Lease.
a822	George Bunn ...	N. E. of Salt Creek ...	24	12 0 0	12 0 0	June 30, '74
824	Robert Lawson	Padthaway N. ...	6	5 0 0	7 0 0	"
826	Geo. Boothby	N. E. of Salt Creek ...	25	12 10 0	12 10 0	Sept. 30, '74
827	T. & E. Hull ...	Tatiara ...	10	5 0 0	5 0 0	"
829	James Foot ...	Do. ...	10	5 0 0	5 0 0	Dec. 31, '74
843	George Hayes	Mt. Monster ...	27	13 10 0	13 10 0	Sept. 30, '74
845	D. Gollan ...	Nr. Maria Creek ...	7	5 0 0	2 18 4	June 30, '74
846	George Bunn ...	Two Wells ...	33	16 10 0	16 10 0	Sept. 30, '74
849	Edwd. Stark ...	E. of Monster Mt.	31	15 10 0	15 10 0	"
850	Do. ...	Do. ...	19	9 10 0	7 18 4	"
863	Thomas Hardy	E. of Marcullet	20	10 0 0	8 6 8	"
872	Robert Lawson	Padthaway ...	14	7 0 0	7 0 0	June 30, '74
874	Do. ...	Do. ...	7	5 0 0	3 10 0	Sept. 30, '74
887	John Morphett	Gosse's Hill ...	126	63 0 0	52 10 0	Dec. 31, '74
902	J. & A. Cooke	W. of Monster Mt. ...	42	21 0 0	19 5 0	Sept. 30, '74
912	A. S. & J. H. Clark ...	E. of Winpinmerrit ...	8	5 0 0	4 0 0	Mar. 31, '74
913	Robert Lawson	Padthaway N. ...	18	9 0 0	9 0 0	June 30, '74
914	Bryan Cussen	Bangham ...	32	16 0 0	16 0 0	"
915	D. McArthur ...	W. of Hundred of Killanoola	13	6 10 0	7 11 8	"
962	Theode. Hull ...	S. E. of Monster Mt. ...	22	35 0 0	13 15 0	Dec. 31, '74
963	James Brown...	Avenue Range ...	15	61 0 0	7 10 0	Mar. 31, '75
964	Do. ...	Do. ...	43	78 10 0	21 10 0	"
967	J. & A. Cooke	Wly. of Monster Mt. ...	34	17 0 0	18 8 4	Sept. 30, '73
980	Alex. McArthur	Marcullet ...	25	12 10 0	12 10 0	Mar. 31, '74
981	D. McArthur ...	W. of Hundred of Killanoola	7	5 0 0	4 1 8	June 30, '74
982	J. W. Lea ...	E. of Lacepede Bay ...	53	26 10 0	13 5 0	"
983	George Ormerod	W. of Marcullett ...	60	30 0 0	12 10 0	"
986	John Livingston	Isle of Dogs ...	10	5 0 0	5 16 8	"
989	Peter Roberts	E. of Lacepede Bay ...	14	7 0 0	8 3 4	"
990	Walter Rogers	Do. ...	6	5 0 0	3 0 0	"
991	Robert Lawson	Padthaway, N. ...	9	5 0 0	6 10 0	"
993	T. W. & J. H. Boothby	Reedy Well ...	17	8 10 0	9 18 4	Sept. 30, '74
998	T. W. & J. H. Boothby	Do. ...	36	18 0 0	19 10 0	Dec. 31, '74
1000	Peter McDonald	Do. ...	17	8 10 0	9 18 4	Sept. 30, '74
1001	Edwd. Stark ...	S. W. of Monster Mt. ...	46	23 0 0	26 16 8	"
1004	Step. Jeffrey ...	Callendale ...	11	5 10 0	5 10 0	"
1006	Ormerod & Stockdale	Woolmit ...	3	5 0 0	1 15 0	"
1007	Dond. McArthur	W. of Hundred of Killanoola	4	5 0 0	2 6 8	Mar. 31, '75
1008	New & Clark ...	Adjoining Conkar S. of Tatiara	16	8 0 0	8 0 0	"
1014	Peter McDonald	Witalara ...	10	5 0 0	3 6 8	"
1015	A. Scott ...	Witalara ...	8	5 0 0	2 13 4	"
1041	T. & J. Dodd ...	Coorong ...	3	5 0 0		"
1070	T. W. & J. H. Boothby	Nr. Reedy Well ...	12	6 0 0	2 10 0	Dec. 31, '75
1072	Edwd. Stockdale	Lake Hawdon ...	4	5 0 0	1 6 8	Sept. 30, '77
1095	George Young	Coolatoo...	4	5 0 0	2 10 0	Sept. 30, '76
1096	Walter Rogers	E. of Lacepede Bay ...	28	14 0 0	5 16 8	"
1097	W. J. & J. H. Browne	Do. ...	72	36 0 0	15 0 0	"
1107	Harding & Bunn	Lake St. Clair ...	2	5 0 0	0 8 4	Dec. 31, '76
1136	Philip Levi ...	N. E. of Fifty-six-mile Well ...	119	59 10 0	24 15 10	Dec. 31, '74
1173	A. S. & M. S. Clark ...	S. of Monster Mt. ...	53	26 10 0	11 0 10	Mar. 31, '75
1174	Do. ...	N. Ely. of Border Town ...	43	21 10 0		Dec. 31, '78
1175	Do. ...	Do. ...	25	12 10 0		"
1190	Wm. S. Douglas	N. of Tatiara ...	40	20 0 0	11 13 4	Sept. 30, '88
1214	J. G. J. Ker ...	Tilley's Swamp...	6	5 5 0	2 10 0	Sept. 30, '89
1222	H. S. Price ...	} E. of Chinamen's Wells ... {	34	17 17 0	9 18 4	Sept. 30, '89
1223	Do. ...		46	23 0 0	13 8 4	Sept. 30, '90
1224	Do. ..		45	22 10 0	13 2 6	"
1225	Bryan Cussen...	Bangham ...	40	20 0 0	8 6 8	June 30, '75